John O'Farrell has published four best-selling novels, two comic history books, a political memoir and three collections of his popular *Guardian* column. His books have been translated into around twenty-five languages and adapted for film, TV and radio. In a previous life he wrote for TV shows such as *Spitting Image* and *Have I Got News For You*. He recently co-wrote the Broadway musical *Something Rotten!* and (with Nick Park) the next film from Aardman Animations.

A long-standing season ticket holder at Fulham FC, he followed them from the bottom division to the Europa League final and fully intends to follow them all the way back down again.

@mrjohnofarrell

WHAT THEY'RE SAYING ABOUT

'As **hilarious** as it is spot on'
MAIL ON SUNDAY

'A tart narrative voice and a delectably understated way with wisecracks... **very very funny**'
NEW YORK TIMES

'**So funny** because it rings true... packed with well-observed jokes'
THE TIMES

'A **rare treat**... Hilarious and heart-tugging, a memorable comedy'
GUARDIAN

JOHN O'FARRELL

'The one-liners are sublime
and the comedic situations
utterly hilarious. Don't miss this'

DAILY RECORD

'A **splendid satire** for our
celebrity-hungry age'

DAILY MAIL

'Punchline-fuelled, relentless humour.
Giggling several times a page
with plenty of out-loud
laughs is guaranteed.
IS John O'Farrell funny?
Very'

MIRROR

BY JOHN O'FARRELL

FICTION

The Best a Man Can Get

This is Your Life

May Contain Nuts

The Man Who Forgot His Wife

There's Only Two David Beckhams

NON FICTION

Things Can Only Get Better

Global Village Idiot

I Blame the Scapegoats

I Have a Bream

An Utterly Impartial History of Britain

An Utterly Exasperated History of Modern Britain

Isle of Wight to get Ceefax (editor)

There's Only Two David Beckhams

John O'Farrell

BLACK SWAN

TRANSWORLD PUBLISHERS
61–63 Uxbridge Road, London W5 5SA
www.transworldbooks.co.uk

Transworld is part of the Penguin Random House group of companies
whose addresses can be found at global.penguinrandomhouse.com

First published in Great Britain in 2015 by Black Swan
an imprint of Transworld Publishers

A CIP catalogue record for this book
is available from the British Library.

ISBN
9781784161392

Typeset in 11/15pt Giovanni Book by Kestrel Data, Exeter, Devon.
Printed and bound by CPI Group (UK) Ltd, Croydon, CR0 4YY.

Penguin Random House is committed to a sustainable future
for our business, our readers and our planet. This book is made
from Forest Stewardship Council® certified paper.

1 3 5 7 9 10 8 6 4 2

For the Snakepit Strollers

*(The team of true gents I've played football with,
every Tuesday night, for the last twenty-five years.)*

'They think it's ~~all over~~ not starting'

England v Germany – World Cup Final

Lusail Iconic Stadium, Qatar – 18 December 2022

Back when I was at school, the careers advisor asked me if I had any private hopes or dreams.

'Definitely!' I said. 'England winning the World Cup.'

'No, I mean like *personal ambitions*, something you could achieve yourself, through your own efforts?'

'Oh sorry, I see what you mean. Yeah; *be there* when England win the World Cup.'

I had considered this dream to be a rather mature one. My previous fantasy had featured me scoring the winning goal; I used to kick a plastic ball against the garage door while improvising TV commentary in which I was the hero of the ultimate game; *'And here comes Alfie Baker on the edge of the box! He beats a defender, he beats another, he shoots, he misses, he breaks the greenhouse window!'*

When I realized I would never be England's greatest player, I resolved to be their greatest fan; I would get a job where I could follow the national team around the world and write about how consistently fantastic England were. What could possibly go wrong with this plan? But then of course, after so many decades of disappointment, England finally did reach their second-ever World Cup final.

So much has been written about the most outrageous month in the history of football, the bizarre twists and turns of that scandalous tournament, that you might think there's nothing you don't already know about Qatar '22. My own account may not win the Samuel Johnson Prize for Non-Fiction like John Terry's did.* But I was right there in the middle of it all; from England's failure at Russia 2018, through their unconventional qualification for the tournament and the incredible story that exploded on the day of the final. This is what really happened back in 2022.

Just as I'd always hoped, I was indeed seated in the stadium at three o'clock, though it was not quite the perfect view I'd always pictured for myself during all those sleepless nights that I'd worried this day might never come. At the time of the scheduled kick-off, I

*At least I'm pretty sure John Terry won it. He was certainly in the photo.

found myself staring at the coat hook on the back of a toilet door. There are certain times when you desperately want to be alone. This one came along when I was in a packed 80,000 all-seater football stadium.

Earlier that day, I had taken my allocated press seat along with all the other sports reporters from around the world, watching the Lusail Iconic Stadium gradually fill up and wondering how they could have grown such perfect green grass in the middle of a desert. (Answer: they didn't, they had it flown in from Poland.) The facilities were lavish, the technology was state of the art, the atmosphere was – well, air-conditioned. Even the food laid on for us had been carefully planned to cater for all nationalities, with haute cuisine prepared by a Michelin-starred French chef, fresh lobsters flown in from Canada and probably some reheated meat pies somewhere for the English. No luxury had been overlooked in the furnishing of this hi-tech temple to sport in the middle of nowhere. Built specifically to host the 2022 World Cup final, it would never be this full again. So it was a shame that the match it was built for might not actually go ahead.

Around the world in bars and cafés, a billion football fans had been really looking forward to watching the dream final. And back home in towns and villages from Cornwall to Cumbria, St George's flags were hanging out of bedroom windows; kitchen chairs had been carried into living rooms to accommodate the extra viewers gathered round especially purchased wide-screen TVs. Parents and their children had pulled on replica England shirts, roads had cleared, shops had closed, Scottish people were pointedly taking their dogs for a walk.

Those of us in the press pack had got wind of FIFA's announcement before it reached the crowd and TV viewers around the world. Initially, the game was to be put back by one hour, pending an emergency board meeting. Rumours began flying around the stadium that the World Cup final was secretly already cancelled, but they just hadn't announced it yet to avoid starting a riot. The official statement referred to 'suspected irregularities'; and if FIFA thought something was a bit dodgy, then everyone understood it must be way off the scale.

Of course the whole world knew what they were referring to; the incredible scandal had broken over-night. 'How typical of the British tabloids . . .' said one pundit, 'to release a story timed to do maximum damage to their own team's chances of winning the ultimate prize.' With no idea whether the game would go ahead or not, live TV coverage had continued and commentators had been forced to keep talking, while cameramen desperately scanned the stadium, trying to find anything of interest to keep the viewers' attention.

'And there we see the players' water bottles, lined up and filled . . . with . . . water. Water of course, very much a precious commodity in this part of the world; the peninsula, being as it is, very much . . . a desert. Barry?'

'Very much so Ron, and all credit to the ground staff here in Qatar, because the pitch looks very well watered; no brown patches or indeed vast areas of barren sand with nothing but cacti; despite as you say, the very desert-y conditions that are typical of this part of the Saudi peninsula – um – so, yes, let's have another look at highlights of that third-place play-off . . .'

Qatar 2022 was always going to be a controversial tournament, long before members of the USA team started feigning injury for exactly five minutes in the middle of each half to allow for commercial breaks back home. It was the first World Cup which saw a few players changing their names to well-known global brands for advertising purposes (though this rather backfired when iPhone was sent off for head-butting Pepsi). But all of these aberrations had been reported in England with an amused tolerance, as if these eccentric incidents were merely a quirky sideshow to the main story of the Three Lions' triumphant progress.

Because, as so often, any sense of moral outrage at a sporting scandal soon dissipates if your own team is doing well. In fact, the closer we got to the final, the more we became convinced that this was possibly the fairest and most impeccably hosted World Cup ever.

But all that changed with one British newspaper's front page on the morning of the final. After all the scandals leading up to Qatar 2022, it seemed that somehow the greatest controversy had been saved until last. The final itself might be cancelled. The England team looked like they would be disqualified and sent home in disgrace. The very country that had invented the game might be about to finally kill it off at the worst possible moment.

The air-conditioning in the toilet gave out a constant gentle hum; it was the only noise I could hear in a stadium still packed with football fans. I looked at the time on my phone – fifteen minutes had passed since the match was supposed to have started. I pressed the screen to check the news; of course it was all about the scandal and the resulting uncertainty. For the sake of trade relations with this oil-rich state, major world leaders had accepted invitations to Qatar and were here for the showpiece final. Even President Clinton was in the stadium and said how disappointed she was. 'I really hope this situation can be resolved and we see Great Britain play-off in the Soccer Games World Series . . .'

I rang my eleven-year-old son's mobile; I could picture him sitting at home, still hoping to watch the match. He dropped my call. I stared at the bowl of pot-pourri next to the scented soap dispenser. That's not a detail you see very often in toilets of the football grounds of England. And then I put my head in my hands. I wondered if I might just hide out here until everyone had gone back home and completely forgotten about the 2022 World Cup.

Thinking over the events that had led me here, I realized I had actually had two personal ambitions in my life. One was to see England win the World Cup. The other was to make it as a football reporter for a national newspaper. I had never imagined that one day I would have to choose between the two.

'You don't know what you're doing!'

Norwich City v West Bromwich Albion – Premier League

Carrow Road, 12 May 2018

Suzanne left me for an MK Dons fan. I support AFC Wimbledon. If you cannot appreciate why this break-up was more painful than most, you are probably reading the wrong memoir. Now her boyfriend takes my son to watch MK Dons. On my weekends, I take him to watch AFC. In decades to come, I fear he will be recounting all of this to his therapist.

I should admit, however, that Suzanne was not the first to have an affair. I had been in an emotionally abusive relationship with football since long before we met. Mistress Football had promised me excitement, romance, even ecstasy on occasion. In reality it was all tense between us; there were raised voices, mood swings and extended sulks. Like so many supporters of lower division clubs, I kept hoping to compensate for the lack of quality and glory at club level by slavishly following the national team. All around Wembley you see our flags draped over the hoardings; 'Dover Athletic', 'Gateshead FC', 'Stalybridge Celtic'. We go to more internationals than Premiership fans because all we ever get in lower league football is ungainly kick-and-run and continual disappointment. Whereas with the England team – well you can finish that joke off yourself.

I had first met Suzanne on a sunny Saturday in June between the end of the play-offs and the beginning of the European Championship. It was an unbelievable year; Greece won Euro 2004 and AFC Wimbledon won their first promotion and the Premier Challenge Cup. Suzanne was quite into sport herself; in her youth she had played hockey for her county despite the ball being much too small and the players being allowed to carry sticks.

We were together for six seasons on and off. Suzanne and I didn't fight because she felt I loved football more than her, or anything clichéd like that. But finally she said she wasn't sure she wanted to spend the rest of her life with someone '*so passive*' which, looking back, I probably should have responded to in some way. 'It's like you use being a fan as an excuse not to take re-sponsibility for your own life. You leave it to twenty-two football players to dictate your mood.'

'Not true!' I said. 'There's also substitutes, the officials, two managers plus all the fans . . .'

That didn't get a smile either.

'You always follow the path of least resistance, Alfie. Maybe it's because you let yourself be consumed by something completely outside your control. But just once in your life, I'd like to see you make one difficult, definitive decision.'

'OK, well maybe we should split up,' I said, which was the only example I could think of.

'I agree. I think you're right.'

'No, I only said *maybe*. I don't really think we should split up . . .'

'See, there you go again. Putting off the hard choices. Well, I'll make this one for you. It's over!'

A couple of months later she got back in touch to tell me she was having a baby and that I was the father. I suggested that was a good reason for us to get back together; to get married even? That's when she told me about the new man in her life.

I said if she'd let me, I would like to play an active role as the baby's real dad. And that turns out to have been the best decision I ever made. Pretty soon I realized I would do anything in the world for my son; I would lie in front of a train for him, I would fight a great white shark; even if he asked me to support another football club – well, *obviously I'd never do that*, but I was constantly thinking about him, saving him football souvenirs and freebies, always thinking 'Tom would love this'.

Soon after he was born, I did a postgraduate sports journalism course, I started writing stuff for fanzines and websites, I wrote non-league match reports for local papers. And in the years that followed I rose steadily, from the lower leagues to the very top, like Wimbledon FC, though thankfully I wasn't forced to change my name or move to Milton bloody Keynes. Back then, I had believed that football had integrity. I aspired to write about it with integrity, always hoping that one day I might get to cover that ultimate game.

I had not had another proper relationship since I had split up with Tom's mother; and in recent years even my love affair with football had become tarnished. Of course we all change over the years, but the beautiful game had transformed beyond recognition since we'd first become hitched. It felt like a sport in crisis, a bubble that was about to burst.

Nothing illustrated this more clearly than the infamous Norwich versus West Bromwich Albion game on the last day of the 2018 season. On the face of it this had seemed an ordinary game at the lower end of the table. For a couple of years in a row both clubs had barely avoided the drop into the abyss; the ultimate catastrophe that is being cast into the second tier. For these two clubs, like most in the Premiership, there was never any chance of winning it; the purpose of every season was simply to try and stay where you were. It was as if the only ambition for the yachts in the America's Cup was *not to sink*.

Fortunately these two particular sides were already safe by the final Saturday and so Norwich and West Brom could play out this match knowing that they had survived another year. Except a terrible misfortune had crept up on both teams without them realizing until now. They were joint top of the Fair Play League. Disaster! Whichever side came out of this afternoon's match with the best disciplinary record would have to enter the qualifying rounds of the Europa League at the end of June. Neither club could afford the squad for this sort of campaign; the team would be crocked and knackered by Christmas and relegated in May. Thus it suddenly became absolutely essential to the survival of both clubs that they allow their opponent to finish above them in the abstract league no one had been watching. In short, this final match of the season was now about getting more red and yellow cards than your opponents.

With the players still warming up, I wandered over to the buffet in the press hospitality section. The chicken curry was stone cold. Strange? The rice was floating in tepid water. There was nothing even remotely edible on offer. 'Of course . . .' I thought. The Fair Play League also takes other factors into account such as the professionalism of the non-playing staff and the welcome at the ground; there were dozens of ways for a club to lose points and slip down the table.

'Erm . . . excuse me, is there anything else to eat?' I asked politely.

'Fuck off!' barked the catering manager.

She could see I was a little taken aback.

'Are you from UEFA?' she whispered.

'No – press. The *Mirror*.'

'Oh, OK, sorry. We're under strict orders. I'll bring you something out of the kitchen if you promise not to write that it was nice.'

All credit to the Norwich manager – he really had thought of everything.

It was an unusual game from the outset. Never before had I seen a club captain celebrate winning the toss by removing his shirt and running to embrace the fans. The perplexed referee was forced to show the Albion captain a yellow card before the game had even kicked off. The Norwich players looked annoyed, but I think this was only because they hadn't thought of that. The match got underway and from the centre circle, the ball was passed back to their big centre back who launched it into the air. Two opposing midfielders leapt to win the ball, but only one thought to give himself an extra advantage by raising his arms into the air and catching the ball with both hands.

'Handball!' went the shout. Except the appeal came

from all the offender's teammates. The referee had blown his whistle and looked ready to reach for the yellow card. But the opposing midfielder was arguing with the ref: 'You can't book him for that, ref – that was just ball-to-hand, it was totally accidental!'

'He *caught* it and was still holding on to it when he landed . . .'

'No way, you can't book him for that, ref! You . . . you fucking bald shithead!'

And so the first red card of the game was issued with less than a minute on the clock.

The game continued in this vein for ninety minutes, with twenty-one yellow cards, three sendings-off on either side, red cards for both managers and a particularly foul-mouthed Norwich ball boy. It was the most entertaining 0-0 draw I have ever witnessed. Pundits sometimes talk about doing dangerous tackles right under the referee's nose, but this was the first time I had ever seen a player go flying in with a two-footed tackle on the ref himself. The Norwich physio came rushing on for the injured man in black, and to huge cheers from the Carrow Road faithful, stood above him squirting the water bottle in his face. He got a yellow card as well, to more cheers from both sets of fans.

While everyone else on the pitch seemed to be experimenting with other sports such as rugby, kung fu and kick-boxing, one tenacious West Brom player stood out by still managing to play some creative and intelligent football. He reminded me of a young Bryan Robson, with an incredible work-rate and great movement on and off the ball. Unfortunately, like Bryan Robson, he also seemed particularly prone to injury. Running up to take a throw-in, he was tripped up by the giant canary mascot and dislocated his shoulder. He simply got the physio to pop it back into the socket and ran back on to the pitch. But then he stumbled and twisted his ankle and had to limp off. A Norwich defender was mistakenly booked for causing this second injury; initially outraged at the injustice of it, he suddenly remembered he was *supposed to be getting booked* and got high fives from all his teammates for his extreme good fortune.

At the full-time whistle there was a mass brawl; police attempted to separate the two managers while Delia Smith was detained for throwing eggs at the linesman. They were of course free-range organic eggs; you could tell from the deep orange colour of the yolk in the linesman's hair.*

---

*For the record, the two teams recorded so many cards that they were both overtaken in the Fair Play League by Stoke. The Potters played their first Europa qualifying game on 30 June in Latvia, and during July flew to Moldova, Cyprus and the Faroe Islands. They were relegated the following season at an estimated cost to the club of around £60 million. And all because their captain had neglected to punch a single opponent.

Like all the other hacks present, Bill Butler from the *Sun* was already well into his piece and barely looked up from where he was already furiously typing: *Disgrace! Shame of overpaid thugs as football hits a new low.* He bemoaned what sort of role models these violent cheats could possibly be to our youngsters and demanded that the players should be forced to donate a whole year's wages to charities for 'British kids'.

It pained me to know that he was being paid to go to Russia 2018 while I'd be forced to write my match reports from in front of the TV back home. I hated the way Bill wrote about football. If there was a breakdown of acceptable conduct on the pitch, he was certain about the amount of tolerance that should be afforded this sort of behaviour – 'Zero'. No other number was ever mentioned, I could never have haggled him up to 'three tolerance', maybe ending up somewhere about '1.5 tolerance'. It was 'zero' right from the outset, that's how strongly he felt about it. He was 110 per cent sure of that. Not 73 per cent sure like me.

If a game was being played somewhere around the end of October, you could guarantee his match report would say something like: *Halloween came early to The Hawthorns where Albion's defence was a horror show for the home fans. It was trick or treat all night with the visitors tricking the West Brom goalie, and treating themselves to a couple of goals before the break, after which, horror of horrors, the Albion centre back ghosted the ball into his own net.* His match reports were created automatically by a special sports writers' word processing software called Microsoft Hack. You simply fed in the teams, the scorers and the date and the software wrote the article for you. *The Liverpool defence seemed to think it was still Christmas Day as they gift-wrapped two goals for the next-door neighbours in this ding-dong not-so-merry derby. It was a case of the post-Christmas blues for the reds, who'd clearly had too much pudding – the turkeys were well and truly stuffed here today. With the summer break approaching, Liverpool already had their mind on the beach,* ('Help, the software is malfunctioning!') *though there were plenty of fireworks and this fifth of November won't be a night to remember as they made a bonfire of the record books* ('Help, it's jumping all over the place!') *while there was no love lost between these two teams in this Valentine's Day massacre.*

Norwich versus West Bromwich Albion was a match at which Bill fed the clichés 'Rated 18', 'Ugly Scenes' and 'Disgrace to the Game' into his computer, and the morally outraged match report reliably wrote itself.

But for me, that farce of a match crystallized the crisis of the modern game. All the FIFA corruption scandals, the establishment of the Premier League, ordinary fans priced out of the stadiums, Qatar; it all came down to one obvious thing. The world of finance, or profit and loss, or put simply 'money' had engineered a hostile takeover of football and stripped out the unpredictable 'sporting' element. Here, for example, was a European cup competition that both sides desperately *didn't* want to play in. The black hole of the Premiership sucked everything else out of their football universe. It wasn't just the money; the meaning of other competitions disappeared, the self-respect of the lower leagues was destroyed.

There was no worse fate in sport than a football team being cast into the oubliette of the Championship, probably to face debt, dwindling crowds and the ignominy of getting just twenty seconds on *The Football League Show* when everyone's falling asleep on the sofa. *'Charlton scored first at the Valley with a penalty scored by that blonde Polish girl you fancy from the sandwich shop – yes, you are having a dream, you should have gone to bed when* Match of the Day *finished.'** It remained a mystery to me why victorious players were still given medals, that Premiership winners were presented with a cup. They should have held aloft an enormous cheque, their players should have done a lap of honour waving wads of cash.

So that is what I said in my write-up of Norwich City

*They briefly tried putting lower league football on before *Match of the Day*. But people still couldn't stay awake watching Crawley 0 Barnet 0.

v WBA. That the sport had sold its soul; that most clubs outside the Champions League elite were only there to make up the numbers. Like the team of white guys who played the Harlem Globetrotters, they only existed so that the rich superstars had someone to beat. I wrote that this was the true meaning of 'football violence'; the slow asphyxiation of our national game. I pressed 'send' and waited for the reaction back at the office.

My boss at the paper had not been sports' editor for very long and was perfect for the job apart from the minor detail that he knew nothing whatsoever about sport. Hugo had been thoughtlessly promoted into this job when the shrinking newspaper had merged its showbiz supplement with sport. He would regularly say things like 'Could you file some copy during the interval?'

'The "interval"? You mean "half-time"?'

'Half-time, yes. And lots of colour, you know: what the audience are saying, things like that . . .'

'The audience? You mean, *the crowd*?'

Surely a man of the arts such as Hugo would welcome such a philosophical piece, even in the *Daily Mirror*? I paced up and down in the hospitality suite at Carrow Road, which was just as well because the staff were still not taking any chances and had loosened the screws on all the chairs. Delia Smith had taken the trouble to learn all the German swear words and was now directing them at UEFA's Swiss observer. He was actually a French speaker, but she probably knew that too. Still no word from the office, so I thought I would begin my journey home. I passed the referee seated on the stairs, his head in his hands, still only halfway through his match report.

On the walk back to the car I felt my phone vibrate in my inside jacket pocket.

'Alfred, it's Hugo.' He always called me 'Alfred' instead of 'Alfie'. It's one of the things they teach you at journalism school; always get everything *slightly wrong*. 'Everyone here is talking about your piece. Your writing is like no one else's.'

That could mean anything I thought. I was still expecting him to explain why they couldn't run it.

'We're giving it a double spread. It's knocked the Manchester v Derby game off the back two pages.'

This wasn't the time to tell him the other game was a Manchester *derby*, not Manchester v Derby. County were still in the Championship.

'Wow – thanks,' I said.

'So, listen, have you ever fancied going to the World Cup finals to cover England?'

He said that like it was a totally left-field idea that might never have occurred to me.

'You really mean that? Me going to the World Cup to follow England?'

'I'm filling out your credentials right now. Your writing is a breath of fresh air, Alfred.'

I punched the air like I had just scored the winner at Wembley. The next day I worked out England's likely route to the final and researched all the Russian stadiums and cities I would be visiting if the optimistic predictions on my home-made wallchart came true. Suddenly I was feeling less disillusioned about the beautiful game. Of course, my take on the controversial match had not precluded someone else back at the news desk knocking out a back page under the headline 'Animals!' which declared that it was *time to show zero tolerance to the overpaid soccer thugs*. But I was gratified that the *Mirror* had published my rant in full on the inside pages, word for word. Or *almost* word for word; the reference to West Brom's number 7 reminding me of a young Bryan Robson had been cut.

It struck me as curious that more obvious edits hadn't been made. I didn't mind particularly, I was too experienced a hack to be indignant about a little trim like that. But just out of curiosity I mentioned it to Hugo, and then to the subeditors, and they were quite insistent that none of them had made this edit themselves.

Maybe it was some sort of computer glitch, I told myself . . .

'He kicked it hard on purpose'

Junction Juniors v Bellevue Boyz
Under 8s Little League
Bishops Common – 9 June 2018

'Oi, Alfie, what would be your All-Time Greatest England XI?'

I looked up to see my flatmate arranging old football cards on the kitchen table in a manner clearly designed to stop me doing any work on a Saturday.

'Mark, I'm trying to get this World Cup piece finished here actually . . . Did I mention that I'm going to the World Cup to cover England?'

'Yeah, but help me out here; if you could select the greatest ever England football players and put them all in the same team . . . who would you pick?'

'No.'

'What do you mean, "No"?'

'I'm not getting into this again. It's one of those pointless discussions that wastes hours and hours going round in circles with no bearing on anything real or meaningful. Like what would you do if you won the lottery, or what would've happened if Hitler invaded Britain?'

'Well we'd all be German and we might win a few more penalty shoot-outs. OK. We won't talk about it . . .' he said, looking a little hurt. 'I'll just do my selection in private . . .'

Mark had hundreds of old football cards that he had collected down the years and was clearly pleased to have found a new excuse to dig them out. He sometimes mocked the fact that I had kept my old Panini sticker album, despite the fact it only had two cards in it, both of them David Beckham.

'There's Only Two David Beckhams!' he had sung all day when he'd first discovered it.

Now he took his own David Beckham card off the table and replaced it with a player I struggled to recognize.

'Right, if I put Carlton Palmer *there* . . .' he mumbled to himself.

'Carlton Palmer?'

'Sorry?'

'You can't have Carlton Palmer as one of the greatest ever England players.'

'I thought you didn't want to talk about it.'

'I don't. I'm just saying. You're only picking Carlton Palmer because you're a Sheffield Wednesday fan.

There is no objective measure by which Carlton Palmer ever qualifies to be in the All-Time England XI . . .'

'So who would you put in that position then?'

'I wouldn't. Because I am not taking part in this discussion. Just not Palmer – Steven Gerrard? Or Frank Lampard maybe?'

'In the same team? Wouldn't they overlap?'

'No, because I'd play Gerrard deep, to release Lampard as a goal-scoring midfielder. If I was designing this team. Which I am not.'

'OK, fine.' Mark affected an air of private study again. 'So let me see . . . left-midfield. Ryan Giggs . . .'

'I know what you are doing.'

'What?'

'Trying to get me to respond. We both know Giggs is Welsh.'

'He played for England Schoolboys . . .'

'Because his school was in England. He got like sixty-something caps for Wales. You can't have Ryan Giggs. Who've you got up front? Pelé?'

'So who would you put at left midfield?'

'Well-it's-traditionally-a-problem-position-for-England-but-I-have-to-say-that-I-think-you-could-play-Bobby-Charlton-there-ahead-of-Tom-Finney-with-Ashley-Cole-at-left-back-giving-you-good-cover-if-Charlton-drifted-towards-Lineker-in-the centre . . .'

And that was it – Mark had me hooked, just as he

had intended. The next two hours mysteriously disappeared into a sinister time vortex in which a pointlessly academic conundrum with no correct answer was debated back and forth and no work was done for the rest of the morning.

The two of us had moved in together as a temporary stopgap arrangement about a decade earlier. Mark's girlfriend Jenny always complained about the smell and had bought him a bowl of pot-pourri, which contained dried petals and pine shavings, and more latterly old cigarette butts. Perhaps we should have talked about whether we were both a bit too old to be sharing a messy flat with a World Cup wallchart pinned above the telly, or whether I was seeing enough of my seven-year-old son. But first we had to get to the bottom of this important business of who should be captain of the All-Time England XI: Bobby Moore, Billy Wright or Kevin Keegan.*

It was just a few days until England's first match in the 2018 World Cup, and the subtext to this seemingly pointless conversation was 'I am really worried about

---

*We finally agreed on Bobby Moore. With Keegan there's always the danger that he'd resign the captaincy and threaten to quit the game if he heard someone in the crowd tutting at him. 'I don't have to take this!' he'd fume at the press conference afterwards. 'When I overheard that tut and looked round to see that so-called fan raise his eyebrows; I'm not prepared to stand there and take that sort of abuse!'

our first game . . .' and my subtitles would have read, 'Me too, I really think we can start with a win, but I don't want to tempt fate by talking about it.' According to the wallchart on our fridge, three points against Morocco and then we'd end up topping the group and avoid meeting our bogey-team Germany in the round of 16.

'So who would you have in goal?'

'Gordon Banks; got to be.'

'No, see I'd go for Seaman.'

'Why on earth would you pick David Seaman over Gordon Banks?'

'Well because Banks is eighty-something and half-blind. That's going to be a problem in a penalty shoot-out.'

'Ha ha.'

In fact, I was anxious about two football games that Saturday. The advent of the World Cup had fired up the enthusiasm of Tom's classmates, and today was the day he and his friends would play their first ever competitive football match. Every weekend, I had come up to the common with my excited son, and for a chaotic hour or so lads and dads had played together; passing, running, dribbling, with each of the fathers doing their very best to demonstrate fair play and good sportsmanship while madly competing with each other to set up their own sons for an easy tap-in. The game required the adults to pull off the difficult balancing act of letting the little boys beat them in tackles and shots, but never allowing it to appear so obvious that the boys felt patronized. 'You let that in on purpose!' was expressed with the same outrage as 'You never let us score'.

And now some of the dads decided this World Cup might be a good time for the boys to form themselves into a proper team and play against other kids of their own age. This proposal had been greeted with universal enthusiasm and the boys all wanted to wear their brand-new replica England kits. I had to stop myself objecting on the grounds of negative symbolism. Was it only me who felt privately panic-stricken about starting this World Cup by watching lots of little England shirts running around chasing the ball with no idea what they were supposed to be doing?

I think father and son could sense one another's nerves as we headed up to the common together. Tom said nothing, his head down; concentrating, worrying, maybe even silently praying. I was nervous because I so wanted him to love it. We lived apart, he was growing up away from me; I was counting on football to be the bridge between us. Finally as we spotted his teammates, he shared his private thought with me.

'I really hope I get a goal.'

It's hard to find that balance between encouragement and realism.

'Well, no, Tom, you're playing goalkeeper . . .'

'I know, but sometimes goalkeepers get goals?'

'Er, well *sometimes*. But your job is to stop goals. As a rule, the very best keepers don't keep going all the way up to the other goalmouth during the game.'

He looked a little disappointed about this. As it turns out, he did score a goal. You want to support children at each stage of their journey. Step one, they score a goal. Step two, they try and score it at the correct end.

I had started the day by working out the all-time greatest eleven players ever to pull on an England shirt. Now I was watching the team that was surely the all-time worst. You watch a seven-year-olds' football match with a different set of anxieties. For example, at no point when '1966 England' got a goal kick did anyone worry that Gordon Banks would struggle to kick the ball hard enough for it to roll out of his penalty area. At which point one of several burly opposition strikers would be waiting like coiled predators to blast the ball straight back into the net. Unlike the World Cup winners, Junction Juniors FC conceded quite a few of their goals like this. It was a set piece that Bellevue Boyz had obviously been working on in training. 'Listen, when their puny keeper passes the ball straight to you from a goal kick, just boot it as hard as you can back in the direction of his goal.'

Nor did the fans at Wembley have to worry about one of the England players forgetting his football boots and having to play in his sandals. Junction's left back actually had to wear someone else's plimsolls, which were about two sizes too big and flew off every time he went to kick the ball (which admittedly was not very often, given the way the possession statistics panned out).

I wanted to tell off the horrible boys from the opposition for being so mean to my son; why were they picking on this goalkeeper by repeatedly scoring goals? Tom's stoicism as he picked the ball out of his net made me love him even more, but somehow I felt like this was all my fault, I had let this disaster happen. In my head I imagined the TV pundits analysing this match:

'If we look at little Baker there in the number one shirt, he makes a basic goalkeeping error of turning and cowering as the striker shoots on goal.'

'But he still manages to partially block the ball, which strikes him on the side as he turns away, before it rolls slowly into the net to make the score 6-0.'

'Baker clearly badly injured by the ball there, Barry, as he goes down in a scream of agony, with his dad having to come on with the magic sponge and a cuddle.'

'Yes, the goalkeeper later complained that the striker *kicked the ball hard on purpose* – does he have a case, Barry?'

'Well it's hard to tell from the replay. But FIFA are going to have to look at this; I mean, if players are deliberately kicking the ball *hard on purpose*, it could lead to a lot of seven-year-olds getting quite badly hurt.'

Mark wandered down from the flat to join me on the touchline, smoking a roll-up fag, and generally looking as if this game was not a particularly big deal.

'How they getting on?'

'They're losing six-nil.'

'You must be infected by some rare type of bird flu, most prevalent in brightly coloured talking birds such as macaws and cockatoos?'

'Yes, I am sick as a parrot.'

Mark always did this. Today it was just annoying. Another goal rolled past my son and the opposition had the bad manners to celebrate it.

'Bad luck, Tom! Nothing you could do about that one!' I called out. Every time a goal went in, Tom looked straight to me to disallow it for some contrived reason and then seemed to exhibit an enormous sense of injustice each time this didn't happen. Mark relit his skinny cigarette.

'Hmm . . . I think I may have spotted your team's early tactical mistake.'

I didn't respond; I wasn't in the mood to accept criticism right now.

'Being middle-class.'

'What?'

'Look at them. All in brand-new England kits. The other team can't even afford matching T-shirts. That should have been a clue?'

I affected a scoff at Mark's simplistic analysis, but deep down I'd known we were in trouble from the moment I saw that our opposition spelt 'Boys' with a 'z'. Tom's team were all pampered privileged boys, kept indoors all weekend, their only sports practice a ten-minute kick-about with their dads, who would shower them with praise for even managing to connect their foot with the ball. 'Oh you've scored AGAIN! You clever, clever boy!' Middle-Class-Dad would exclaim, as he let the ball roll slowly between his legs, 'You really are the best footballer ever in the history of the whole-wide-world.'

Meanwhile on the other side of town, that seven-year-old working-class kid was probably halfway into the second hour of a twenty-a-side kick-about with mostly older boys barging him off the ball and into the mangled wire fence, till he learnt to barge back at the right moment, or swerve or shimmy, with his big brother shouting at him to stop chasing the ball and get back into position.

Tom and his friends had a rude awakening when the first proper opponents they came up against did *not* accidentally fall over at the first shot on goal and then say 'Well done, that really was a very, very good shot; let's go and tell Mummy what a super-duper footballer you are . . .'

At half-time the boys gathered round their coach in a state of shock and disbelief that the other team could have been so unsporting as to *try*. Toby's dad, the self-appointed team manager, proceeded to give them a half-time team talk of which I'd estimate the kids understood approximately three words. Little faces stared up at him blankly as he gabbled statements like 'Jamie, if they get a corner, go screener, then drop deep, play off of midfield, and knock it into the overlap. Tom, make sure your guys don't spring the offside trap early doors, demand cover – I want to hear you demanding cover, understand?' Poor Tom nodded in a way that showed he clearly didn't. The coach might as well have told the seven-year-olds, 'Now listen, a quark is an elementary particle and fundamental constituent of matter, yeah? Quarks combine to form hadrons, the most stable of which are protons and neutrons, the components of atomic nuclei – right now, remember that in the second half!'

There was at least some sort of consistency and symmetry to Junction's game. They let in seven goals in the first half and seven goals in the second. Perhaps their preparations should have involved less time rehearsing goal celebrations.

After the final whistle, Toby's dad gave the boys a dressing down about their attitude and then resigned as their manager after just one game. He 'had taken the team as far as he could' and 'it was time for the club to enter a new chapter'. The other parents all turned straight to me.

'Alfie, you know all about football, you should be in charge . . .'

'What? I can't be manager – it's the World Cup, I've got to concentrate on football. No offence, lads.'

'That's OK – England will be home again after three games, so that's settled then; Alfie is the new manager of Junction Juniors FC . . .'

Nearby, Mark was ironically applauding the decision.

'We never agreed on the manager . . .' he said as he came over.

'What do you mean?'

'For the All-Time England XI. Who do you think: Alf Ramsey? Bobby Robson? Or maybe you?'

'Very funny. I'm doing it for the boys. For Tom.'

I looked across to where my son was gathering his things, his brand-new goalkeeper's gloves, his brand-new zip-up training top, his England water bottle – I'd already invested a small fortune in his football career. Some of his friends had started a kick-about but he didn't seem inclined to join in.

'We don't have to go straight off, Tom. You can play a bit more footy with your friends if you like?'

'No thanks, can we just go home?'

Nearby some crows were fighting over the leftover crusts of the boys' half-time croissants. And then Tom said the worst three words he could have said.

'I hate football.'

All's fair in love, war and the World Cup bidding process

England v Germany – World Cup Round of 16

Spartak Stadium, Moscow – 3 July 2018

No one could quite remember at what point in the twentieth century the accepted rate for how much a team should 'Give It' had gone up from 100 per cent to a 110 per cent. Never mind that this was actually mathematically impossible; it remained the universally accepted rate of 'Giving It' across all media. When footballers' autobiographies were published on Kindle, the end of the book said '110 per cent'.

But then in the 2017–18 season, something shocking happened. One manager claimed a higher level of effort for his team. It was a minor Tuesday-night cup match between Crystal Palace and Wigan that might have gone unnoticed but for the provocative statement given by Wigan's acting Director of Football after the game: 'We're obviously totally gutted to have gone out early doors, but I can't fault the lads for effort, they gave it 120 per cent.'

There was a gasp from the interviewer.

'Sorry – how much did they give it?'

'The boys was legend tonight. To give it 120 per cent like that, well you can't ask for no more.'

But pretty soon managers *were* asking for more. The following week coaches were telling their players to give it 130 per cent, within a month it had risen to 140 per cent. Analysts were predicting that Giving It inflation could hit a totally unsustainable 150 per cent by the time of the World Cup; '*Good evening, here is the* Six O'Clock News *from the BBC. The world of football has called for urgent government action this evening as "Giving It" inflation hit a record 182.7 per cent. The crisis has spread to other European leagues, with one report from Portugal of managers claiming their players had "given it" a staggering 212.7 per cent, despite calls from the German Bundesliga to set a European standard for Giving It.*'

In the end, boom was inevitably followed by bust and as the season came to an end, players were giving it just 55 per cent. Or only 40 per cent, when it came to England's performance in the 2018 World Cup. This was the tournament that England had once thought it might have a chance of hosting. In 2010, England had needed twelve votes out of twenty-two to bring football back to its historic home. The Football Association were confident that they might actually pull it off. They had done the groundwork, they had put together an excellent bid, and they had private assurances from a large number of delegates. They got one other vote and were eliminated in the first round.

Two winners were announced that day; 2018 would be hosted by Russia. And the 2022 World Cup would be hosted by . . . And then Sepp Blatter sneezed or coughed or something, because a strange noise came out of his throat. Oh no, apparently that was the name of one of the bidders. Who? 'Guitar', that's a musical instrument, isn't it? So there was a double whammy for English football fans that day. Firstly that England's 2018 bid had utterly failed, and to add insult to injury, it would seem that we were not as capable of hosting a World Cup as a stringed instrument of the chordophone family.

We had carelessly allowed ourselves to believe that we had put a pretty good case for why we should host the finals once again. We had the stadiums, we had the transport infrastructure, we had the football fans. We even thought it worth mentioning that we actually invented the sport back in the late 1800s. 'Really?!' gasped all the other FIFA delegates, 'You never mentioned that before, England! All this time we had presumed that the sport had naturally emerged in the early Bronze Age along with pottery and fur bikinis, and now you finally tell us that football was an English innovation! Well you really should have mentioned it earlier . . .'

Despite the sledgehammer sarcasm of the FIFA delegates, England had no idea that we had gone around bidding for the World Cup in completely the wrong way. Delegates were arriving in shiny new Bentleys with Qatari number plates; climbing out of the back seat with beautiful Muscovite escorts on either arm. Qatar and Russia were offering massive bribes and inducements, while the English were handing out FA fact sheets featuring old photos of Stanley Matthews.

'Stop distracting me!' said one particularly short, fat delegate to the Russian prostitutes in the back of his new Rolls-Royce. 'I'm trying to read all about Villa Park's convenient transport links.'

'Oh, I would have loved to take your leaflet featuring lots of ethnically diverse children at Wembley Stadium. But unfortunately my hands are already full with these two large suitcases stuffed with banknotes.'

By 2015, it looked as though the audacity of their corruption might finally be catching up with them. Leading figures in FIFA were arrested, Sepp Blatter resigned, and football fans hoped this was the beginning of a long road back to some integrity in the world's favourite sport. But there were too many divisions, still too many vested interests to recommence the bidding for 2018 and 2022. It was felt, on balance, that it was probably not worth provoking Vladimir Putin into declaring war on the Western powers that had questioned the existing arrangements.

It would be wonderful to recall how England made up for failing to host the 2018 World Cup by going on to win it in style. That the country that was humiliated in the bidding process for 2018 came first where it mattered: on the pitch itself. But when England drew their opening game 0-0 against Morocco, the supporters started to experience a foreboding sense of déjà vu. The Moroccan team was not packed with footballing superstars from the Premiership or La Liga. The TV commentator said things like, 'And fans of the Premiership might remember Papa Ouaddou from his brief spell on loan at West Ham.' Or, 'François Demele knows the English game a bit; he once had trials for Bolton.' We had the most nervous defenders since the ostrich in *Bedknobs and Broomsticks*. The midfield were even worse, it was like watching a conjuror repeatedly building up to an amazing trick, but every time he got to the climax, he would drop the top hat, or there would be no rabbit inside, or the lady really would have been sawn in two. Actually, that's probably too horrific. That's more how England played in their second game. South American 1970s-style haircuts are so much more annoying when they are celebrating a goal against

England. Paraguay went 1-0 up in the second minute, and England seemed content to leave it at that. We did eventually manage an equalizer ten minutes from full time, with a penalty 'brilliantly dispatched by the England captain'. The penalty was replayed over and over again on British TV – it was the only time I ever saw England score five penalties in a row.

I had missed out on Brazil 2014, with its carnivals and sunshine and rum cocktails. Instead here I was in Smolensk in the drizzle, with England giving performances as dour and joyless as Russian passport control. I knew I was very lucky to have this job, and that I really shouldn't complain about lousy catering or trying to find a compatible Russian modem plug after the hotel wireless had gone down again and they were screaming for my copy back in London. But unlike the other journalists, I *cared*. The other hacks all remained neutral and impassive because only with such reptilian cold blood could they utterly destroy those England players when they refused to deliver the results. Bill Butler said to me once, 'You're not a journalist; you're just a fan with a laptop.'

Despite the disappointing first round, England still managed to come second in the 'Group of Death' (so-called because that is what it felt like to watch the matches). Now they faced the winner of Group B in the next stage. 'Ah, but now that they are finally playing world-class opposition . . .' went the eternal optimism, 'England will finally raise their game and peak when it matters most.'

But I was not over-brimming with hope as I took my seat in the Moscow national stadium that grey day on 3 July 2018. England were up against their age-old footballing rivals Germany. 'Rivals' in the way that Bury might consider themselves local rivals with Manchester United. Since losing to England in the 1966 World Cup final, Germany had been in fifteen major football finals. England had not been in one, managing only two semi-finals, both of which were lost to . . . ooh, I can't remember, the name of the winning semi-finalists escapes me.

During the group stages, England had experimented with various shapes from 4-4-2 to 3-1-4-1 (which didn't even add up properly). But in the game against Germany their formation was simply '11'. Even the goalie seemed unsure which part of the pitch he was supposed to stand on. The game was cruel in every way possible. Germany scored early on – a slick passing move through the centre of midfield that had our defence looking as rusty as the hinges on England's trophy cabinet. Germany looked solid in possession for the entire first half, scoring a cleverly worked second, with England reduced to gracelessly hoofing long balls up the field to where their striker would have been if they had bothered to agree this tactic in advance.

At half-time, England's chances of winning the World Cup weren't quite dead, but relatives were gathering at the chances' bedside. England's chances were gently asked if they would like to see a member of the clergy and if there were any overseas bank accounts they hadn't previously mentioned.

After the restart there was a brief moment of optimism when England got an undeserved goal to put the game back within reach. But I always think it's a mistake to score against the Germans, it only annoys them. Their big centre forward went back up the other end and got a third and then a fourth. Without making a conscious decision to give up hope, I realized I'd revised my private target down from an England victory, to merely hoping this rout would not be too utterly humiliating.

The TV cameras had stopped cutting to David Beckham watching in the crowd; now that things were going badly they cut to Vladimir Putin instead. The Russian leader was sharing a chuckle with his Minister for Sport, probably claiming it was sheer coincidence that he'd annexed the bits of Ukraine that just happened to have all the best football players.

In the Spartak Stadium England fans were growing angry. Some of them were swearing and shouting at the players that they had been relying upon to transform their lives. Of course, deep down furious football fans are actually angry about other stuff, they just need a way to let it all out. They really ought to scream 'Oi, ref, you twat, my menial job is unfulfilling and underpaid!' or 'Oi, linesman, my wife left me for Alan and it's your fault, you bastard!'

At the beginning of that game there had been two versions of the newspaper ready to print the next day. One file was marked 'Heroes', the other was 'Zeroes'. And all my stories had been dutifully prepared for the positive background stories on the victorious England players. The wives and girlfriends who gave them support behind the scenes; reports on the visit to a local Russian school. Who'd want to read about all that now? The readers back home would be feeling furious and betrayed. They wanted scandal, they wanted their anger channelled; they didn't want to hear about how the England captain played football in the dirt with some local schoolchildren (even if he did dive for a penalty and get an eleven-year-old sent off). So none of my stuff was in the paper that week. And when the paper's World Cup coverage was slimmed down after England's exit, I was recalled to London. I'd been knocked out of the World Cup for not playing dirty enough.

In an attempt to remain positive I wrote a seemingly

innocuous piece about the next generation of England players that gave us all hope for the future. *Kicking Images! It's the England Legends Tribute Team!* In fact I was going public on a nagging set of coincidences that had been growing on me all season. In addition to the resemblance between the young West Brom midfielder and Bryan Robson, I had spotted other youth team players that reminded me of great stars of the past. There was the Newcastle United midfielder who got the yellow card which put him out of the FA Cup final. He burst into tears on the pitch, but when the Toon went on to win it without him, he'd cheered up enough to don a pair of plastic breasts on the open-top bus. He definitely reminded me of someone, I was sure it would come to me soon.

I pitched this article idea to my editor, who did his best to look like he had the faintest idea what I was talking about.

'What, and you have an entire England fifteen for this?' asked Hugo.

'*Eleven*, Hugo. There are eleven players in a football team.'

'Of course, sorry. We only did rugger at my school. Hated it! Hid in chapel the whole time, reading the Romantic poets.'

But he was persuaded that an optimistic profile of these young England hopefuls would be the perfect antidote to the anticlimax of the World Cup, plus it was always worth finding some excuse to print a big picture of Bobby Moore holding up the Jules Rimet trophy. 'Make it fun!' he exclaimed, clapping his hands together like the director of a Broadway musical.

In fact I'd not had as many as eleven names, but the process of writing up this feature started to persuade me that it must be more than a string of bizarre quirks of fate. Watching David Beckham beside footage of the current number 7 in United's Under 19s, Gary Lineker next to Leicester's young centre forward; it made me shiver with the ghostly peculiarity of it all. Each one of them was signed to the same club as their predecessor, in the same position, at the same point of their careers. Only the faces were different; the physique, the height, their mannerisms, everything else was the same. I pulled these curious observations together, thinking it would never add up to anything more than a diverting novelty feature towards the back of the *Daily Mirror*. 'I'm making something out of nothing,' I tried to tell myself.

And then the government stepped in to have the feature pulled.

Ultimate team

All-Time England XI v 1970 Brazil

On Tom's Xbox – 6 July 2018

With England knocked out of the World Cup had come the usual ritual of trying to decide which country to support now. Mark had been leaning towards the hosts, Russia, since they had never won it before and there was a Russian defender at Sheffield Wednesday.

'You can't support Russia!' I'd protested. 'They are a deeply authoritarian country; abusing human rights and stirring up unrest in Ukraine and Chechnya . . .'

'Yeah, but great writers; Tolstoy, Dostoyevsky . . .'

'Have you read a single book by any of them?'

'I am familiar with Chekhov . . .'

'Yeah, from *Star Trek* . . . What about Portugal? They've never won it.'

'Nah, can't quite forgive them for their messy withdrawal from their empire; Angola, Mozambique, East Timor . . .'

'All right, what about Spain?'

'Sure, great football players, but as a nation aren't they a bit too cruel to animals? I mean there's probably a part of rural Andalucía where a Spanish victory would be celebrated by getting the fattest man in the village to sit on an old donkey.'

'Well there's not many countries left. Germany? Italy?'

'No way!'

'What? What? Because of the war?'

'No, no – that's forgotten; that is all water under the bridge . . .'

'Why were you such a definite "no" then?'

'Because . . . well because they have both won it too many times before. Yes. Nothing to do with the war. And I'm not supporting bloody Japan either. But World War Two is of no concern to me whatsoever. I'm supporting the boys from Brazil!'

'You do realize the origin of the phrase "The Boys from Brazil", don't you? It's a 1970s thriller about an evil plot to clone lots of Adolf Hitlers.'

'Now that would make for an interesting team! Eleven players with the name "Hitler" on the back of their shirts: *And there's the audacious right-winger Hitler celebrating his hat-trick with his trademark one-arm salute to the crowd! And in an eerie parallel with the Ardennes in May 1940, the French simply have no answer to Hitler's aggressive policy right down the middle.*'

Our important discussion was interrupted by a call from my work – and I found myself standing up when I discovered I was talking to the Editor-in-Chief.

'Alfie – we've had to pull your piece. I got a call from DCMS – the Minister himself. They invoked Leveson – said we'd overstepped the mark.'

'But that's ridiculous! It's just a little novelty feature.'

'I know, but most of the players you featured are still minors. They said it was an invasion of privacy. Did you do anything to provoke such an extreme reaction? Did you doorstep them? You didn't hack their phones, did you?'

'No! I simply noticed something about them and wrote about it. How can they cite Leveson for that?'

'It's because they're still kids. I can't make a stand against the government over a stupid thing like this, so I had to give way. It made the first editions but then it was pulled, website and all. I think they're trying to flex their muscles and they landed on this.'

He hung up and I stared at my handset for a moment, which I thought only happened in bad films. It made no sense. Why would the Minister for Sport take action late at night over an article about some youth players most people had never heard of? Mark had an explanation: 'Maybe it wasn't the Minister for Sport who intervened? Maybe it was the Minister for Preventing Alfie Printing Total Bollocks?' Mark was not particularly convinced by my fascination with the England Youth Team.

'Of course some footballers are going to remind you of other footballers,' he said. 'That's like saying one rugby player must be connected to another because this one also stood on the bar, pulled down his trousers and poured a pint of bitter over his head.'

He was in the middle of picking his team for a match of FIFA 2018 on Tom's Xbox which I kept at my flat for when my son came round. I think Tom had used it once. Today I was going to be 1970 Brazil, whereas Mark was going to waste another hour by selecting his All-Time England XI. EA Sports had painstakingly programmed in pretty well anyone you could name who'd ever pulled on an England shirt. That's *as a player* obviously; the millions of lager-swilling fans with replica shirts failing to hide their beer bellies were not included. You wouldn't have wanted Fat Phil, that van driver who plays darts for the Rose and Crown playing up front with Bobby Charlton and Gary Lineker. But there was something both miraculous and absurdly decadent about the fact that millions of pounds of software programming had gone into bringing this perennial pub conversation to life. Now we could actually see them playing together, we could choose from hundreds of all-time heroes down the decades; and watch the avatars of Jimmy Greaves and Tom Finney and David

Beckham passing to each other on our TV screens. You could even select retro commentators, so Mark always picked a female linesman and then chose Andy Gray and Richard Keys, just to listen to them being really sexist about her.

'There must be something they're hiding . . .' I said to myself, still reeling from the phone call.

'So if I have Tony Adams next to Billy Wright at the back . . .'

'Why would an article about England's Under 19s set off alarm bells in the corridors of power? What could they possibly be trying to hide?'

'And then I put Stanley Matthews on the wing laying the ball off to Gerrard in the middle . . .'

'I mean, what is it about those players that is so special? What is it that I could be overlooking?'

'Ashley Cole at left back. Has to be.'

With the benefit of hindsight, some things are so blindingly obvious that it's impossible to imagine that the facts didn't occur to anyone at the time. It's like Edwardian England *must* have known that the *Titanic* was going to sink, because every costume drama set in 1912 features men in hats meaningfully announcing 'I am off to America on the *Titanic*. They say it's *unsinkable* you know!'

'Hang on, you're the third person to say that to me today. I'm starting to smell a rat here.'

'Nonsense. And I'll tell you something else: there'll be no war in Europe in our lifetime . . .'

So it was with the incredible news that was to rock the world of football in 2022. None of us saw it coming and yet the clues were there for all to see. Obviously after the event, a hundred different commentators claimed they'd harboured private suspicions all along. But the truth is that nobody predicted it, precisely because the idea itself was so extreme and ridiculous.

'There,' said Mark. 'I've got all the greatest England players in the same team. Now let's see if they can beat the boys from Brazil.'

The intervention of the government had transformed my idle curiosity into something of an obsession. Like a parent saying 'Don't look in our bedside drawer', it immediately made it the only place you wanted to look. I had come to accept the fact that I was never going to be the sort of journalist who was interested in sniffing around for salacious gossip on celebrity footballers. But the idea of actually *investigating* something, to harbour vague suspicions and so dig further into a mystery; that seemed to me to be a worthy pursuit for a newspaper reporter. Obviously it had been many decades since newspapers had stopped funding time-consuming research based on nothing more than a hunch. Investigative journalism was now limited to following lots of celebrities on Twitter and then concocting an entire story out of whatever they might have chosen to reveal in 140 characters.

But I had resolved to start digging. I thought the most obvious place to start researching was press interviews and club profiles to see if any significant clues about them could be gleaned from what was already out there. 'Hmmm . . . interesting,' I thought, chewing my pencil as I considered this new evidence. The *OK!* magazine interview with the brilliant young Geordie I was researching revealed that his favourite food was 'steak and chips', and his favourite pop star was 'Ed Sheeran'. On the club website's profile, I uncovered the clues that his favourite drink was 'Pepsi Max' and that his dream car would be a Lotus Elise S.

This was gold dust! How could people claim that the in-depth psychological cross-examination was dead? Frost with Nixon, Oprah Winfrey with Lance Armstrong, the tradition continues . . . I could picture the scene as the hardened interviewer played her subject like a mouse; alternately flattering him, un-nerving him, winning trust, probing, cajoling before finally forcing the young footballer to break down in tears and confess: 'Yes, yes, all right, I admit it. My favourite holiday destination is Ibiza and my all-time top movie is *Spiderman*.'

My suspicions were heightened by the fact that none

of these players seemed to have the usual stuff in the archive. I had put in a search request at the paper's cuttings library, but bizarrely there was nothing. Every overpaid young player normally has a folder full of old stories about when they first signed for this or that club, the first huge pay cheque, the tragic split with the original girlfriend from back home the following week. But not one of this lot had crashed a sports car at the age of seventeen; it was most irregular.

What I needed was to talk to the players myself. But a standard email request to Newcastle United had simply met with the curt response: 'We regret that the player requested is not available for interview at this current time.' This was from the 'Media Relations Team' whose job it seemed was to be rude to people from the media. Undeterred, I tried a different tack with another player on my list and contacted his agent. 'We regret that the player requested is not available for interview at this current time.'

Exactly the same wording. Two players with different Premiership clubs represented by different agents; so why would an everyday request for a press interview be immediately rejected with an identical phrase? As a control in this experiment, I telephoned Newcastle United to enquire about interviewing another player, far more famous and experienced than any of the youngsters from my original list.

'Sure, Alfie . . .' they said, sounding friendly and helpful. 'Oh, in fact he's right here, do you want to do it over the phone now?'

'Oh no, it's OK, thanks. I've changed my mind, I don't want to interview him any more . . .'

I was not going to be so easily deterred. Nothing was going to put me off the scent. I got myself a blank piece of paper in order to list all the ways I could think of to uncover the secrecy surrounding the players on my list. 'Right . . .' I said to myself, adopting the steely determined look I'd seen in that film about the Watergate reporters. 'OK. Right . . .' and I stared at the wall for a while.

Ten minutes later I was wondering how Bernstein and Woodward ever found out anything without Google.

Foundation myths

England U19s v Australia – Commonwealth Games
Eden Park Stadium, Auckland – 28 July 2018

'And there we see the sky father Ranginui symbolically embracing the earth mother Papatuanuku and quite literally creating life itself, as it were . . .'

That summer, the Commonwealth Games were held in New Zealand, and I had felt privileged to watch two British sports pundits improvising a live commentary over the opening ceremony and the re-creation of the Maori foundation myth.

'Marvellous to see these traditional painted wooden masks, a lot of them have their tongues sticking out, don't think that's meant to be rude . . . different cultures . . . different meanings . . . for tongues . . . And many of these designs date back thousands of years, of course . . . traditional . . . crafts . . . And you can buy little ones at the airport . . . So a good present idea there . . . And now here comes their son, this is Tane, I think. Yes, this is Tane! Son of Ranginui and Papatuanuku, of course – and now the son is pushing earth mother and sky father apart . . . typical kids! And this is the moment when he throws the stars into the sky to give light; there goes the sun and the moon there; more a symbolic representation of the moon I think; the moon not literally a star of course, as we now know, but obviously the Maoris didn't have telescopes before the Europeans arrived—'

'They didn't have anything, Barry – complete savages!'

'Er, well, they lived a simpler life, didn't they? And who's to say which is best?'

'Weren't they bloody cannibals? And I'm sorry, Barry, but all this sticking your tongue out, where I come from, that's just disrespectful. And if I'd pranced about like their Haka before a game, my old man would have given me a clip round the—'

'Ha! Yes . . . well, not too many Maoris in Dudley, I guess.'

'Not when I was growing up there weren't. But now there's bloody all sorts . . . I tell you what I'd do—'

'OH AND THERE IT IS!' cut in Barry. 'Light is created! Tane has played a blinder! Ron – wonderful foundation myth, wouldn't you say?'

'Oh, it's a great story, Barry, sure. But as a scientific explanation for how the universe and that came into being, it's complete rubbish. But yeah, all credit to these Maori fellas for putting on a good show. Always fun to see these primitive legends re-enacted for us by the local ethnics.'

The Commonwealth Games Foundation had had the bright idea of adding football to the list of sports represented at the Games in the hope that it might raise the profile of the whole occasion. They'd somehow imagined that dozens of world-class football players would eagerly fly right round the world to play in New Zealand during a narrow gap they'd spotted in between the World Cup and the beginning of the Premiership season, and for the first time in its history, the Commonwealth Games might be something that people took an interest in.

'What is Common Wealth Games?' asked Chelsea's Italian manager.

'Well, it's a bit like the Olympics. But without all the countries that beat us in the medals table.'

Of course none of the major British, African, or Caribbean stars were ever going to be released by their clubs. The eleven best players from the Falkland Islands all turned up, but were easily beaten by Tuvalu (which is in fact a real country and not a Vic Reeves catchphrase). But for many of the youngsters who were still plying their trade in the reserves, it was a great way to get some tournament experience. So it was that the England Under 19s were sent to represent their country and really began to gel as a team. The FA thought they had found the perfect solution to their youth development programme. They needed the talented England Under 19s to get some competitive games under their belt. But they wanted the youngsters playing their matches away from the media spotlight. This is why the Commonwealth Games had been perfect. Until they went and won it.

I suppose I should have felt a degree of pride that youngsters I had been regularly singling out for praise in my match reports were now being noticed by everyone else. But it was actually very annoying to see Bill over at the *Sun* pretending to be the first person to notice these great talents and copying my call that they replace the England team proper at the next World Cup.

Interest back home grew with each game as this team got all the way to the final by beating older, more experienced teams from Nigeria, Northern Ireland, Ghana, Jamaica, South Africa and the newest Commonwealth member Qatar. In a refreshing contrast to the lethargic old guard who had flopped out of the World Cup, this England team were winning by playing attractive, positive football and the fact the team was made up entirely of teenagers caught the imagination of the public back home. The possibility of England actually winning a tournament had clearly not occurred to the suits of the Football Association, but with England in the final they made the sacrifice of flying first class to New Zealand during a particularly wet and miserable month back home.

Mark and I watched this late-night kick-off round at our flat with half a dozen friends and acquaintances who loved us for our many qualities such as our massive wide-screen TV, our comfy chairs and the mini-fridge beside the sofa that was used only for storing beers. Tom had been allowed to come and stay the night and I could sense he was secretly thrilled to be in this unapologetic cave of masculinity, where no one watched their language or bothered to adjust their slovenly behaviour for his benefit. When Mark called the referee a 'fucking obese wanker' Tom turned to me and asked, 'Dad, what does *obese* mean?' He knew things about players that no one else in the room knew, he shared facts and news about transfers and potential signings.

I think Mark was quite pleased to have my seven-year-old son there, because no one else was laughing at his running joke of contrived literal metaphors.

'And you have to say, John, after ninety minutes, no one could have foreseen a giant pumpkin coach coming on to the pitch being pulled by six white mice dressed as footmen, to take the visitors home at midnight . . . Absolutely, Ron. It's a fairy-tale ending.'

The greater the groans the more encouraged Mark felt to search for another.

'So England have arranged items of bric-a-brac to sell from their fold-out table, hours before the summer fete is due to open . . . Absolutely, Ron, they've set their stall out early . . .'

All of the England players that I had been researching were in this team, which meant that everyone also had to put up with me raising the uncanny similarities again.

'Wow, that's incredible – it's like *The Da Vinci Code* or something!' exclaimed Mark.

'Isn't it?' I said, feeling encouraged.

'So this footballer you think could be secretly related to Paul Gascoigne or whoever . . . This is based on the fact that this England player is also very good at football?'

'Oh, I see; you're being sarcastic . . .'

'And he does not have a particularly highbrow sense of humour? That is too weird to be a coincidence – two professional footballers, both of whom aren't Professor of Philosophy at Trinity College, Cambridge; 'tis a happenstance too extraordinary for one kingdom!'

'It's not just Gascoigne – look at that team. Can't you see it? Nearly all of them remind me of someone else. And I am going to concentrate on— YES!!!'

Our discussion was cut short by a fantastic England

goal; a beautiful pass from midfield, then a perfectly flighted ball right on to the captain's head to put England in the lead after ten minutes.

'What a pass that was! Fulham won't be able to hang on to him for much longer . . .'

'Or maybe he'll always be a one-club man?' I said enigmatically.

'Oh no – who's this one like then? Jimmy Hill? Where's the annoying beard?'

'No. Don't you see it? When I was down at Craven Cottage I thought the statue outside the ground had suddenly come to life and was playing football on the pitch.'

I meant the Johnny Haynes statue, obviously, not that Michael Jackson one they used to have down there. It would have been an interesting midfield if the Prince of Pop had been moonwalking up and down the left wing, spinning around and clutching his crotch every time the ball came near.

'No I don't see it because I am not ninety years old. And I don't spend all my time watching YouTube footage of post-war England teams. How is the book coming along, by the way?'

'Oh, er, slowly. Still mostly notes at the moment . . .'

Mark regularly goaded me about my lack of progress on a book I'd been commissioned to write on the history of the England football team. Originally planned for publication in time for Brazil 2014, it was put back to Euro 2016, then Russia 2018 and the publishers were currently aiming for Euro 2020. But my procrastinating research must have made me more familiar with the playing style of the great England legends than most of my contemporaries.

'I'm telling you, it's uncanny; that shot was pure Jimmy Greaves!'

'And he's wearing an England shirt too! How many different ways are there to kick a football?'

'There's something they're not telling us about this team, I'm sure of it.'

England scored three more goals, looking composed, quick, creative and confident.

'And you have to say, John, that since he scored his hat-trick, Nash has been performing a musical set on a Mississippi steamboat, singing "Ol' Man River" and "Cotton Blossom" . . . Yeah – he's Showboating. There's no doubt about it.'

But the main downside was the non-stop barrage of sarcasm from Mark, saying that every throw-in proved a massive conspiracy of secret offspring and an undercover FA adoption programme.

'What about the goalie, who does he remind you of?'

'Well, it's harder with a goalkeeper, isn't it? There's less to distinguish the way they play; one great keeper is much like another . . .'

At that point England conceded their only goal when a speculative long-range effort was lobbed into the box, and the England goalie was too far off his line and could only watch it loop over his head and into the net. Mark and I looked at one another.

'Seaman!' we said in unison.

Another name was added to my list of players to research. Or rather, 'fail to research'. I had tried to track down the club scouts that had originally discovered these talents and been told that this was restricted information. None of the ordinary facts that might usually be in the public domain were available on these individuals.

I decided if I couldn't get to the team, perhaps I could speak to the man who'd decided to send them out there. Greg Dyke had become the Chairman of the FA in 2013, but had been deeply involved in football for decades. He had been on the board of Manchester United and then Chairman of his boyhood club Brentford FC, as well as having been part of Tony Blair's original inner circle. If anyone could explain the excessive secrecy that seemed to surround these youngsters, it would be this man.

I caught up with him at the PFA Footballer of the Year Awards and managed to win his attention by giving him all the credit for sending the England Under 19s out to New Zealand.

'Thanks. It's Alfie, isn't it – *Daily Mirror*?'

'Wow, you know who I am?'

'Always read your stuff. Used to be a journo myself, of course . . .'

'Yes, well, those young lads give us hope for the future. I've been tipping them for great things for some time.'

'I know you have . . . You were the first!'

Already I liked and trusted him; it's pathetic how effective a little bit of flattery can be. 'But, um . . . I can't seem to get an interview with any of them.'

He sipped his drink.

'Ah well, everyone wants a piece of them now.'

'No, even before, when no one had heard of them. I wrote a piece comparing them to England legends, and the first edition prompted a call to my editor from a cabinet minister, demanding it be pulled! Every interview request gets exactly the same rejection. Word for word. Like it's being orchestrated by a higher power or something . . .' I said, looking him right in the eye and trying to look knowing. He held my gaze for a moment, and then led me to the side by my elbow.

'All right, I'll level with you, Alfie. There is a reason that we are operating a strict media blackout on these lads . . .'

'A media blackout?'

'This is completely off the record, mind . . .' I tried to keep my cool, sipping my drink, then felt some of it run down my chin and on to my shirt. 'You've probably already noticed that these twenty-two youngsters are the most promising English players for a generation . . .'

'Yes. Very much so . . .' ('Twenty-two?' I was thinking inside; I'd only counted eleven!)

'We think they will be good enough to win the World Cup in 2026. But if the media starts to hype up these boys when they're just teenagers, experience has taught us they'll destroy them before they reach their potential.'

Of course I understood that he wasn't including me when he referred to the irresponsible media. I worked for a British tabloid.

'We've invested too much in them to have it all evaporate now. So no press interviews, no nightclub photos, no TV panel shows, no pop-star girlfriends – we're taking no chances. A World Cup victory is too important to this country to let anything get in the way.'

I felt thrilled and slightly disappointed at the same time. It was actually a perfectly rational explanation. Suddenly any vague conspiracy theories I may have been hatching looked ridiculous and all I was left with was a mundane story that I couldn't even print.

'Bastards! They pulled my exclusive about a media blackout! I can't believe it.'

That night I watched the news footage of the victorious team arriving back at Heathrow Airport, and I checked on Twitter to see what people were saying about it all. A mild controversy was being stirred up that there was no victory parade for the 'Commonwealth Heroes', no open-top bus or official reception; the outraged Twitterati couldn't understand why. But I did; I was on the inside, in the know; I'd had it explained to me by the Chairman of the FA himself. In fact, I actually found it quite encouraging to know that the football authorities were finally taking England's prospects seriously. They were thinking long term and ensuring that our future stars were protected right from the outset. As a press man I was supposed to be against things like 'media blackouts'. But as a football fan, I couldn't help agreeing that this might be exactly what was needed.

I stopped plugging these players in my match reports, I stopped asking difficult questions. And somebody must have noticed. Because a couple of months later a collection of secret documents was leaked to me by an anonymous source. There was classified memos between 10 Downing Street and the FA: the minutes of hitherto unknown cabinet committees, extravagant sports science spending projections; a *billion pounds* discreetly pledged to something called 'Operation Early Doors'. It was a top-secret project conceived to 'guarantee' that England would win the FIFA World Cup. And somebody didn't want it to be secret any more.

I've seen 'em given

Junction Juniors v Greens United
Under 9s Little League
Bishops Common – 6 April 2019

Junction Juniors were *'due a win'*. This is football parlance for *'they keep losing'*. 'Junction Losers' (as Mark called them) had now been playing for nearly a year and had never even managed a single point. Call me harsh, but by my logic this meant they were *'due another defeat'*.

As manager I had tried everything to improve their tactical awareness and movement off the ball, to build their confidence and morale. My last post-match reassurance had been deemed 'inappropriate' by one parent who witnessed it. 'You might have lost twelve-nil today against those rough boys off the estate, but let's get things in perspective. You're going to have much nicer lives than them. You are going to get well-paid jobs in a warm dry office. They are going to have to lift heavy objects in the rain. One day, some of those nine-year-old thugs laughing at you may develop poverty-related diseases or become drug addicts from their time in prison. Who are the real losers, boys, eh – them or you?'

'Er, steady on, Alfie,' interjected another dad. 'Better luck next time, eh lads?'

On another occasion I had thought if we filmed the game we could watch it back later and see how the boys might improve their positioning and movement. Since I was required to run up and down the touchline shouting 'Stop bunching!' I delegated the job of camera operator to Suzanne, who often used to come and watch. She did an excellent job, holding the camera steady, following the ball, going in close for free kicks and pulling back to show the shape of the whole game. The only problem with this recording is that she and the other mums were chatting on the touchline.

If the commentary had been from John Motson, we might have heard words vaguely relevant to the pictures, he might have said, 'And a big kick up field from Junction's young goalie . . .' while Mick McCarthy might have chipped in with 'Aye, they're trying to bypass Greens United's midfield, but it just keeps coming straight back to them . . .' But the commentary on this tape brought a whole new dimension to the genre.

'We haven't looked at St Judes Academy; it's a faith

school, and we haven't done that whole going-to-church thing . . .'

'No, neither did we, although Simon is sort of Catholic . . .'

'But their specialism is music, and Johnny does play the recorder . . .'

Young Karim was dispossessed in the centre circle and fell in the course of the tackle but was up and chasing the opposing player headed for the Juniors' goal. Yet the commentator's voice does not seem to register the increase in the drama on the pitch.

'We could go together before Book Club if you like?'

'I'm not sure I can make Book Club this month. Jim's got a work thing, which he only just told me about and of course he presumes it's my job to find a babysitter . . .'

'Oh, Simon's exactly the same . . . I'm not sure I'm going either, to be honest, I only got twenty pages in. Whose idea was it to pick a misery memoir . . .'

Greens United are pouring forward, in the background you can hear dads screaming at the attackers and defenders.

'I think it was Anita, she always tries to be a bit different. Different would be if she cooked for us for once instead of always ordering takeaway and asking for the money – oh was that a goal?'

'Oh, it looks like it, which side scored?'

'Oh dear, I think it was the other team. Poor boys, you have to admire the way they keep going, don't you . . .'

We all know Kenneth Wolstenholme's famous commentary at the end of the 1966 World Cup final, 'And here comes Hurst, he's got . . . Some people are on the pitch, they think it's all over. It is now!' You can't help feeling that this iconic moment might have been slightly diminished if Wolstenholme had said, 'I can give you the number of our babysitter if you want, though she's not local so Michael always drives her home . . . Oh, was that a goal? Which side scored?'

I was guessing that the future England prodigies being developed by the FA did not prepare like Junction Juniors, by spending two hours watching their dads trying to assemble the plastic goalposts. Selection for that team had not been based on which youngsters tugged the hem of the manager's T-shirt the most. Like the very top teams, Junction Juniors did operate a rotation system, only ours was organized on the basis of 'making it fair' and 'letting everyone have a go'. You wouldn't extend this system to other contact sports; you can't imagine the commentators from Murrayfield saying, 'And a key substitution is being made here in this crucial Six Nations decider, as Scotland take off their big prop forward Butch McCleish, to put on nine-year-old Kirsty Johnson because she wanted to have a go . . . And oh dear, she's been knocked unconscious . . .'

So finally I made a controversial decision. For our big match against local rivals Greens United I was going to put out our best eleven, and stick with it. I knew I would endure the wrath of fellow parents whose sons might not get to play. But the only reason I would substitute a player was if I judged it would improve our chances on the pitch. I stuck Charlie in goal instead of Tom, since Tom never caught a ball in his life, whereas that was always Charlie's first instinct when it came towards him in the centre circle. I took rude Matthew off completely and made him a substitute. The fact that I was scared of his mum was not a good enough reason to keep him at centre forward. I said that Matthew might get a run out later if we were comfortably in the lead, which was possibly the emptiest promise of all time.

But a couple of minutes after kick-off, I looked at the players in their various positions and felt a warm glow of satisfaction. We were better. With a little consistency and players getting used to their positions, we did actually string a couple of passes together. We defended. We cleared a ball that was dangerously close to crossing the line. Just as I had promised him, Tom no longer seemed to hate football. And then . . . with five minutes to go, and the score still at 0-0, suddenly there was my son, running into the goalmouth with the ball at his feet . . . He's going to shoot! Is he going to score his first ever proper goal, will this be the moment he falls in love with the sport? Are Junction Juniors going to win a game, with my son scoring the winner and his father's controversial team selection vindicated?

It all happened like it was in slow motion. I don't mean that in a metaphorical sense, *that really is how slowly they played.* A defender lunged for the ball but got nowhere near. But at that moment, perhaps alarmed by the notion of being tackled, Tom somehow stumbled over his own feet and fell flat on his face in the penalty area. The chance was gone. I grabbed my face in anguished disappointment.

'Penalty!' declared the referee, pointing to the spot with a sense of drama that didn't quite match the miniature pitch and little wobbly goals. Dads and substitutes on our side cheered like we had won the cup final. This could mean a goal! Our side, scoring an actual goal!

'I never touched him!' pleaded the defender, close to tears at the injustice of it all.

'Penalty!' confirmed the ref decisively, waving away protests and placing the ball on the spot. Tom had picked himself up and looked anxious about what had happened. I was right behind the goal and he shared his secret with me.

'Dad. He didn't touch me. I just fell over.'

'Well, I've seen 'em given.'

'I didn't dive. I promise I didn't dive. I just fell over.'

'Still, I've seen 'em given. This could be our first victory . . .'

'But it's not fair.'

'Oh, no, I suppose not. But these things even themselves out over a season . . .'

I decided I should move away from behind the net. Scoring your first goal is one of the great rites of passage and a boy doesn't want to look up and see his father grinning at him, giving him the thumbs up, any more than when he kisses a girl for the first time. Although admittedly, I did do that.

Tom stepped up to kick the ball. I could still hear the defender protesting that he hadn't touched him. And then a kick and a split second when I saw the keeper was diving to his left, but the ball wasn't going to his left. In fact the ball was going in a completely different direction altogether. In the entire history of football I wonder if that was the first time a penalty ever went off for a throw-in.

There were howls of anguish from his teammates and the other parents. How could he miss so badly? How could he blow our one chance to win a game? But Tom turned around and ran back into position saying to the referee as he passed, 'He never touched me.'

Tom had missed on purpose! He didn't want to win like that. One of his teammates was now explaining that Tom had said he'd put it out of play because it wasn't a fair penalty and one of them started clapping him. Then the whole team applauded him and the parents of both sides joined in. It made the referee look like a complete idiot, which was one of the best things about it.

The game finished as a 0-0 draw, Junction Juniors' first clean sheet, and our first ever point. Suzanne was on the touchline dishing out juice cartons for Tom and his friends; she was so proud of him for doing the right thing.

'Did you have any idea he was going to do that?' she asked me.

'No, it was a complete surprise! I mean, I do remember telling him about the Corinthian Casuals who disagreed with the principle of penalties in 1891 and so chose to deliberately miss them . . .'

'Hmm . . .'

I was already boring her.

'Well, anyway that's what's so great about the boys doing sport,' she continued. 'It gives them a chance to learn about right and wrong.'

'Absolutely. I mean, it doesn't matter at all that it cost us two points and our first win, because obviously it's far more important to always do the right thing

. . . Although as I say, these things do generally even themselves out over a season.'

She gave a dubious look. Every obsessive man needs someone like Suzanne to be his moral compass; it's not something you can download as an app on your iPhone.

Deep down I knew that it must say something about the ethics of my investigation or its subject matter that I didn't want to tell Suzanne about it. The day before this game I had received a third mystery package about the New Labour government's secret plan to develop a World Cup winning team for 2026. 'Why so far away?' I thought to myself. Why had they planned for twenty-eight years ahead when there were so many other World Cups to try and win before then? This team was being designed long before the players had even been born. The leaks prompted more questions than they answered. It all clearly related to the same secret conspiracy, but there was no definitive explanation of what that actually was. I spread the stuff out on my wobbly Ikea bed. I had been presented with a self-assembly mystery: *Attach Document A to Theory D; locate Players E–L and align with Confidential Cabinet Minutes as illustrated.* Unfortunately the ragged photocopied papers did not slot conveniently together to provide me with a fully functioning news exclusive.

And there was still no clue as to my source; only this drip-drip encouragement to keep asking questions. I was both thrilled and slightly scared to have this stuff in my possession. It felt dangerous, something I needed to keep secret. These latest papers dated back a couple of decades: I felt a pang of nostalgia for the old-fashioned font that would have been used to write words like 'Britpop' and 'Dial-Up Internet'. The subtext of this leak was that there was a direct link between the players I was researching and Tony Blair's first government of the late 1990s. Even if the minutes revealed a certain amount of tension between the PM and Gordon Brown about where the money might be best spent:

STRICTLY CONFIDENTIAL

MINUTES OF THE CABINET, 9 JULY 1998

(CONT.)

7.1 The Prime Minister fully accepted the point that there were four national football teams in the United Kingdom but said there was only one team with any real chance of winning the World Cup, and so it would be unrealistic to try and direct major resources towards any team but England.

7.2 The Chancellor of the Exchequer asserted that Scotland were easily as good as 'bloody

England' but were always drawn in a really impossible group. He claimed that England's first-round draw always pitted them against Canada, San Marino and 'Burkina Fucking Faso' while Scotland would have to play Germany, Italy and Brazil. (NB Subsequent checks by the Cabinet Secretary were unable to find hard evidence of England or Scotland ever having been drawn in these exact qualifying groups and it is presumed that the Chancellor was exaggerating to make a political point.)

7.3 The Prime Minister pointed out his own personal Scottish connections.

7.4 The Chancellor claimed the Prime Minister was about as Scottish as 'Desmond Fucking Tutu'.

7.5 The meeting was interrupted with the Chancellor spilling his water, with a considerable amount of it seeming to land on the face of the Prime Minister, with some splashing on the Deputy PM. Mr Prescott then offered 'to deck the Scotch bastard' and was physically restrained by the Secretary of State for Social Security. Ms Harman appeared to be distressed, and tearfully made the point that 'John' should 'leave it' because 'it was not worth it'.

So if Gordon Brown had not wanted money spent on the England team, Tony Blair would have had to proceed without him? Perhaps all this secrecy started right there? On another scrap of paper was a memo from 'TB' asking 'RW' to set up a working party re England/football. At the bottom was scrawled in biro 'no mention to Gordon or Alastair'. I was puzzled by the initials 'RW' – no former cabinet minister or senior civil servant I could find seemed to fit those initials. It left me wondering if Tony Blair had entered into some secret conspiracy with Robbie Williams, Reese Witherspoon or Ron Weasley.

I recalled being pleased in 1997 when we got a Prime Minister who seemed genuinely interested in football. In the election run-up Tony Blair had been filmed skilfully heading a ball back and forth with Kevin Keegan. You could have never imagined Maggie Thatcher doing that. The camera would have been knocked out of focus in a sudden melee and then it would have cut back to Keegan writhing on the floor groaning and clutching his groin.

Other documents now in my possession revealed how the government had watched with envy as France won the World Cup in 1998. They noted that France's win was the direct result of a conscious political decision by the French government to invest massively in sport. When President Mitterrand came to power back in 1981, he committed enormous sums of money to developing domestic sporting excellence, recognizing that success in international competitions can give a boost to a nation's prestige and self-confidence and opportunities to sneer at the English. And a generation later that investment paid off; two years before their World Cup victory, the French had come fifth in the Summer Olympics Medals Table (Britain had come 36th). The French World Cup winning team went on to become European Champions a couple of years later, while England failed to win a single game. These minutes showed the new Prime Minister repeatedly expressing determination to change all of this 'whatever it took'.

But by 1998 grass roots sport in the UK suffered from the problem that there wasn't any actual grass left. Urban children were turning to other sports, such as night-time stock-car racing with stolen Vauxhall Astras. British children were getting fat and lazy; visiting aunties would say, 'My how you've grown, I remember you when you were only *this* wide.' Motivating millions of apathetic teenagers to take up sports on fields that no longer existed was a complex and mind-boggling political challenge. But England simply winning the World Cup; that would be a visible achievement – that, I now learnt, was Tony Blair's overriding ambition for British sport when he became Prime Minister.

So what could be the link between this secret government committee that he'd set up back in 1998, and the current Commonwealth champions who had all been born a couple of years later? I considered all sorts of bizarre explanations. 'Newcastle's brilliant young midfielder is the secret love-child that Paul Gascoigne never realized he fathered, but his family knew all along and that is why they adopted the baby and raised him in the same way.' Or 'Manchester United's promising young striker plays football just like Bobby Charlton because he is from the same part of the North-East and there is also something in the water up there that makes men lose their hair early and imagine that no one will notice a comb-over.'

None of that would have required a government cover-up. So, ridiculous as it sounded, the hypothesis I settled upon was that the government had persuaded dozens of England's greatest footballers to become secret sperm donors, so that the FA could take the male offspring of David Beckham and Bryan Robson and condition them from Day One to grow into fantastic footballers. Mark was intrigued as to how I thought this would have worked on a practical level: 'How do you persuade Wayne Rooney to wank into a petri dish?' he said. 'It's not like you could rely on any England strikers to hit the target.'

Clearly this was not a hypothesis that I could print

in the paper until I was pretty confident of the evidence. Did the players themselves even know that their offspring were being farmed for football greatness in this way? Did these young prodigies know who their real dads were? Were there hundreds of other kids who had been bred in this manner but who had turned out to play football less like Bobby Charlton and more like Suzanne Charlton?

It all felt vaguely sinister and illicit. My son's highly principled moral stand had crystallized a nagging feeling I had about this investigation. Deep down I worried that England must be doing something unfair. Were England youngsters being built up on secretly developed super-steroids? Had Tony Blair and the FA come up with a way to cheat? Did I want England to win at any cost, or had Tom shown me that sometimes you just have to kick the ball out of play on purpose? Or perhaps this was all irrelevant speculation. Because when even the greatest ever England team faced a penalty shoot-out, surely one of them was bound to miss as badly as Tom without even trying.

The twelfth man

England v Poland – European Championship Group C

Wembley Stadium – 18 June 2020

Following the outrage that had greeted Qatar being awarded the World Cup, FIFA and UEFA became very nervous about awarding major tournaments to *anyone*. They listened to all the different European countries arguing about why they should host Euro 2020 and, too nervous to make a decision, announced 'All right you can *all* host it.'

'What?'

'If you can't agree amongst yourselves, you're just going to have to share it.'

'How the hell's that going to work?'

'Well, it will be held all over Europe. And we'll decide later who gets the semis and the final . . .'

So it was that Wembley hosted England in a tournament for the first time since 1996. Mark noticed the pair of tickets on the kitchen table and happily presumed that the spare one was for him.

'No, tonight is going to be my son's very first experience of watching our national team,' I said proudly, as Mark's face fell.

'Really? On a school night? Is that such a good idea?'

'Your concern is touching. Especially for someone who offered him a Jägerbomb on a school night . . .'

'All those crowds, football hooligans, maybe I should speak to his mother?' In fact I was nervous about taking my son to Wembley to see England, but not for the reasons that Mark was suggesting. England had got off to a poor start in Euro 2020 with two disappointing draws – if they didn't win this evening they'd be out at the group stage, and Tom might be put off watching football for life.

'Why are they not playing any of the youngsters?' I moaned. 'It makes no sense . . .'

I had drawn up a list of the young players who I believed made up the twenty-two-man cohort that FA Chairman Greg Dyke had referred to, and I had Post-it notes and football cards all over the noticeboard in our flat. I'd pinned them up in their approximate positions: goalkeepers at the bottom, strikers at the top. I had printed their photos from the Internet and attached these images to the cards.

All this time Mark had regarded me with pitiful shakes of the head, interspersed with complaints that I had taken down his Sheffield Wednesday towel.

'Why would you have a towel pinned to the wall anyway?' I said. 'A poster maybe, a flag at a push. But a towel?'

'It's the *official* club towel. You can't leave it lying around in the bathroom; that would be disrespectful. I'm not having you coming out of the shower and rubbing your arse against the sacred date of our foundation . . .'

Mark always affected bemused indifference to my obsession, though he found it impossible to ignore once I started pinning all-time England legends to the board as well.

'You've left out Carlton Palmer . . .' he pointed out.

I attached a coloured piece of string between the picture of Gary Lineker and Leicester City's exciting young striker.

'So what's this mysterious connection with this one then? Found a footballer who eats crisps?'

'This kid is a very similar forward who joined the youth team at Leicester City, and is currently being linked to Spurs. A prolific goalmouth striker, he's never so much as got a yellow card. Exactly like Gary Lineker.'

'It's an insane conspiracy theory! If you were going to get the offspring of Lineker and Charlton and Beckham and Billy the Fish to play together, you wouldn't need to keep it secret! But more to the point, it's a rubbish idea! How many great footballers have produced a son as good as them? Jordi Cruyff is only half as good as Johan, Nigel Clough can't drink half as much as Brian!'

'Frank Lampard is even better than Frank Lampard!'

'Yeah, but that might be because Frank Lampard inherited his skill from Frank Lampard, or because Frank Lampard trained Frank Lampard from an early age . . .'

'What?'

'Ian Wright had two sons who went on to play football at the highest level. One shared his genes, the other was adopted. See what I mean? It doesn't work!'

'You're right, it doesn't work . . .' I said, staring at the board. 'You can't have Greaves and Lineker playing up front together. Too similar . . .'

I placed Tony Blair in the middle of the board, along with Greg Dyke and John Prescott, plus a silhouette with a question mark under the initials 'RW'.

'Tony Blair? Does he play in your Fantasy XI as well? Don't tell me; supposed to be a left winger, but keeps drifting to the right?'

'I'm convinced Blair is the Mr Big behind all of this. A billion pounds he put into this project! An untraceable billion quid for something called "Sports Science"! I mean, I would tell you more . . .' I said, affecting an enigmatic air. 'I have my sources. But I am professionally obliged to keep some information completely secret.'

'You mean all those documents in your room? Yup, read them. It's obviously one of the lads winding you up.'

'You went through my secret file?? That said *Strictly Confidential*!!'

'Well you shouldn't leave it lying around under your mattress.'

No matter how many hours I stared at this noticeboard, I still felt that many key pieces of the jigsaw were missing. Deep down I knew Mark was right; the secret offspring theory didn't make any practical sense. Then my imagination would veer lazily towards the default sports scandal involving some sort of performance-enhancing drugs, but that didn't seem to line up with these clues either.

Ideally my enthusiasm for this investigation would have been motivated by a high-minded quest for the truth or a professional ambition to make my mark. But I realized that I only felt inclined to pursue this potential football scandal when England played badly, as if I had been personally affronted by the FA and wanted to get my own back. So it was during Euro 2020. Two disappointing draws from England's first two games had me really fired up about getting to the bottom of this scandal. And then England played one incredible, perfect football match that convinced me that the current England set-up was completely faultless, so why would anyone ever want to rock the boat?

Having my nine-year-old son with me for his first ever international made it even more special. I saw it all through his eyes. The jaunty overture as we began our journey to north-west London; Tom pointing out a sprinkling of other fans in England scarves and tops joining the train at each station, until eventually the trickle became a torrent and he was both exhilarated and slightly scared to feel himself part of something so powerful. There was a bit of a crush towards the end, but one of the fans thoughtfully shouted down the carriage on our behalf: 'Oi! There's kids here, cunts!'

Then we joined the massed ranks ambling towards the stadium; thousands of us swarming along Wembley Way, fans chanting far ahead of us and close behind; touts repeatedly mumbling their 'buying or selling' mantra; vendors selling dodgy hot dogs and unofficial merchandise; Tom was wide-eyed and thrilled by it all. Beer swilled in plastic glasses, steam rose from the packed urinals; he had never seen hundreds of adults being so *unsensible*, singing and clapping and shouting random declarations of footballing patriotism.

I gave Tom some background on England v Poland and the famous 1-1 draw in 1973 that had prevented England from qualifying for the World Cup for the first time ever.* I described the period of soul-searching and introspection on how we played the national game during the 1970s, from which the only noticeable conclusion seemed to be that English players needed to wear much tighter shorts.

Our seats were way up high and the long traipse towards the escalators was an anxious one as I kept checking he was not becoming separated from me in the jostling crowd. But for the first time in his life he was going up a hill where he would appreciate the view at the end. I watched him in that transcendent moment when we emerged into the stadium and he suddenly beheld the vast scale of this setting. The luminous greenness of the pitch under the floodlights, the awesome power of eighty thousand people here for the same reason as us; a noise you can feel on your skin, an atmosphere that catches your breath. There is no greater sight on Earth than that first vision of a packed football stadium at night, and to see it through my son's eyes made it all the more awesome. I said nothing, he said nothing; there was no need.

Down on the distant pitch, men in tracksuits

*In fact England did not progress through a World Cup qualification campaign for twenty years during this period. They had qualified automatically in 1966 as hosts, and again in 1970 as holders. In the 1970s England's repeated failures were mollified by the more successful Scotland not mentioning it at all.

nonchalantly kicked balls the length of the pitch and Tom realized that these were real-life Premiership heroes. The famous players on *Match of the Day* really did exist as real human beings, they weren't fictitious characters or computer-generated avatars. What I loved was the surprise in his voice every time he spotted another player he recognized. It was like, what were the chances that he would be here as well!

He gazed across at the noisier fans behind the goals, and pointed out a giant inflatable beach ball being batted about by the crowd, to huge cheers from whichever section was currently in possession. For the next quarter of an hour or so, the atmosphere continued to build . . . the mosaic of empty seats opposite was nearly completed . . . the portentous music was building to its contrived climax . . . and finally came the moment when the two teams were led out on to the pitch. Then a noise you could have swum through as eighty thousand people rose to their feet as one and Tom could gaze out at the view of . . . well, the coat of the tall bloke standing right in front of him.

'Oh, I meant to say, Tom, if anything at all exciting happens, everyone stands up. So you won't see any goals or major incidents or anything.' The man on the other side of him shot me a smile. 'Unless . . .' I added, 'you learn to jump on to your seat the moment it gets interesting.'

The danger in taking an uninitiated loved one to see a football match is that you cannot guarantee them a satisfying narrative. I could have accompanied Tom to a Disney film or an action adventure movie and be fairly confident that Hollywood would provide us with goodies and baddies and a beginning, middle and end. Football creates its own type of suspense by surprising you with rubbish, disappointing games when you least expect it. How many FA Cup finals of my youth were billed as thrilling climaxes to the whole season, only for them to peter out into lethargic 1-0 victories by the club that was always favourite to win? For this match to be any sort of positive experience for Tom, the home side had to win.

And so when England went 1-0 down early on in the game, he looked at me with a sort of desperate confusion as if something outside the known laws of the universe had occurred. Maybe the referee would rule that the Polish striker 'had kicked it hard on purpose' and award a free kick to the England goalkeeper?

The away goal came early enough for me to persuade myself that this actually would make for a far better narrative when England eventually equalized and then went on and won it. But the goal seemed to have stunned the crowd into silence, and our nervousness spread to the pitch. There were a couple of sloppy moments in defence, back passes were too soft or too casual and England struggled to recover from unnecessary danger. 'God, if we carry on like this, they'll get another one in a minute.' And then, as if I had jinxed it, they did.

Poland won a corner and from the edge of the D their huge centre back came running into the goalmouth and headed straight into the net. The Polish section of the stadium erupted again. Now I could feel Tom really hating them. I wanted to say something mature to my son; to explain that they were merely fellow football fans cheering their own team. Except in that split-second, I have to confess I really hated them as well.

With England 2-0 down came the real but unspoken fear that we were going to lose this match and fail to progress to the knockout stages of the European Championship. This appalling prospect seemed to communicate itself to the England players; now they were nervous and tentative – the midfield were passing sideways, kicking the ball back to the defenders, eager to unload any sort of responsibility. The way they were playing, I couldn't see any way for us to get back into this game. But it was then that Tom witnessed the greatest thing that can happen in football. The home crowd turning the match around.

It started from a small area way up high behind one of the goals. England fans rose from their seats and sang 'Stand up! If you still believe! Stand up! If you still *believe!'* and like a wave of optimism it rapidly flowed in both directions all around the giant doughnut of Wembley. The clatter of thousands of plastic seats flipping up added the percussion to this emphatic English male voice choir, and soon the opportunity to demonstrate your faith reached the section where we were sitting. My son looked up in amazement as he saw me standing up and at the top of my voice begin half-shouting, half-singing *'Stand up! If you still believe!'* with more naked emotion than I care to remember. Tom had never seen his mild-mannered father do anything like this before; in another situation he would probably have been appalled. If it had been parents' evening or the school play and 'Dad' had stood up and started screeching new lyrics to the tune of 'Go West' by the Village People, he would have been scarred for life.

But he intuitively understood what was happening here, and without saying anything to me, he simply stood up, climbed on to his seat and started singing along too. His voice was of course unbroken, but still worth adding his few decibels to the general effort as he joined the other 80,000 England fans, all on our feet, all singing together, a noise so loud that the opposition's families must have heard it back in Poland. *'Stand up! If you still believe! Stand up! If you still believe!'*; there were no other lyrics, we just got louder and louder, and you could see the England players growing taller with the adrenalin that was now pumping through their veins.

Now with Poland's number 9 in possession in the centre circle, Luke Shaw put in a tackle of such determination and skill that he won the ball back even though such an ambitious lunge had seemed physically impossible. It had been sheer force of will that had snatched the ball back; the power of 80,000 people urging him on; and before his opponent had registered what was happening, he was back on his feet and laying the ball off to Oxlade-Chamberlain, who was suddenly two paces faster than his marker down the wing. Two England shirts were flying towards the goalmouth as the ball shot across the six-yard box, the Polish defenders unable to get goal-side, and Welbeck dived and headed the ball so hard that the back of the net was rippling before the keeper had left the ground.

And we discovered that our repetitive song actually had a chorus of mad screaming cheers and a special dance in which our arms instinctively flew above our heads as we jumped up and down, and the cheering went on and on until it segued into an ecstatic chant of 'England! England!'

'We did that!' said Tom, turning to me in amazement. '*We* made them better!' He couldn't believe this secret power that we had unleashed against the visiting team, we, the ordinary fans who had just paid to come and watch, we had the ability to transform events on the pitch.

'It's because we said we believed Dad! We said we believed, and it came true!' It was as if after all these years he had suddenly found out that there was such a thing as magic.

The psychology of the match was transformed. Fired up by their goal and the continuing ferocity of the crowd, every England player desperately wanted the ball, determined to beat an opponent with a pass or a run or a tackle. Now it was Poland who looked panicky and disorganized. A speculative shot from way outside the area hit the bar, and England forced a couple of corners and now the tune echoing around the ground was 'Guantanemera!' carefully reworded to suggest that in a minute, we were going to score. Two more England corners; we had to get this equalizer before half-time, before Poland had a chance to change their tactics and take the sting out of the game. But England's goal wouldn't come from a mere corner; this being one of the most perfect games I ever saw, the equalizer had to be something really special. As half-time approached the energy started to slip away and I thought we might not do it. England had the ball in their own half, and no one was particularly making a run or creating any options. Then Harry Kane looked up, saw the Polish goalkeeper on the edge of his area, and launched a speculative shot all the way from the centre circle. It flew in a giant arc, as if following the shape of the iconic arch over Wembley, and with the Polish keeper desperately scrambling backwards towards his goal, it dipped perfectly just below the crossbar as the keeper flailed helplessly, falling backwards into his net where he was joined by the ball.

It was like a complex mathematical calculation, such was the perfection of the elevation, distance, arc, speed – Kane's foot had calculated all of this in the split second that he had looked up and then shot. Like the young Beckham's goal against Wimbledon, or Nayim's last-minute Cup Winner's Cup winner against Arsenal; the ball was in the air long enough for the crowd to think 'What the hell! Did he really think he was ever going to score from there? Oh my god, he might! Oh my god, he has!!!'

England were level and even the Poland fans were applauding. The crowd's rapture had a different quality to it now; of course the cheers were loud and long, but there was a tinge of laughter and astonishment in the mix, followed by the hubbub of chatter all around the ground – it was a goal that made you talk to strangers.

The second half did not produce as many goals, but was no less memorable for it. To qualify as one of the all-time greats, an epic football match also needs a couple of bizarre or comical interruptions along the way. Always a crowd favourite is when the referee gets hurt, and on this night the Dutch official was felled by a misdirected shot at goal which hit him full in the face at what must have been approaching 70 miles an hour. The ref was down for a good minute, and his discomfort was probably made all the worse by the unwritten football law that says that referees are supposed to share a good-natured chuckle about such incidents. But you could see on the giant screen, he didn't want to laugh, he was in real pain. 'Ow fuck!' he kept saying in impeccable Anglo-Saxon. 'Fuck! Fuck! Ow, my face really fucking hurts . . .'

It's strange the way that getting a ball in the face like this never seems to hurt the players. A wet ball can strike a player's nose like a shot from a canon, but a professional will just get to his feet, give his head a shake, and dash back into position. If the sleeve of an opposing player lightly brushed the same part of his face he would be rolling about on the floor clutching his nose in agony.

The next interruption was a little more unusual. I had seen a dog on the pitch before; a squirrel and plenty of seagulls and pigeons (though not all at the same time, obviously – that would be insane). But I had never been at a football match where a rabbit had been the centre of attention for a good five minutes. No one seemed to see where it had come from, but there it was on the big screen, nibbling the sacred Wembley turf, and twitching its nose occasionally, thinking that there was something imperceptibly different about this field. Play was halted and there followed a Benny Hill-type high-speed chase involving most of the players and the match officials. To accompany this farce, thousands of England fans began singing 'Run rabbit, run rabbit, run, run, run!'; a perfect choice only slightly diminished when everyone realized that they didn't know any more words, so they had to keep singing the first line over and over again.

Eventually Poland's enormous keeper managed to grab the hind legs of the now very distressed rabbit, and in one deft movement he swung the poor creature up to his other hand and swiftly wrung its neck, leaving it instantly limp and lifeless. I never heard a packed stadium go so silent.

'What's happened, Dad? Has he killed it?' said my shocked son.

'Er, yes, I think he has.'

'That's horrible,' he said. 'How could he do that?'

One sensed that *Watership Down* had not made quite the same impact in Eastern Europe; the goalkeeper's teammates were now patting him on the back to congratulate him and looked puzzled that booing and hissing was growing from the English crowd. He might have been a highly paid Premiership footballer, but an impoverished childhood in rural Poland stays with you and he gave a thumbs up to the away fans behind his goal who were chanting something in Polish; probably, 'You will certainly have a nourishing pie tomorrow!'

This cultural difference reminded me that Poland was not just a different football team, but represented a whole other country with separate values, traditions and history. Most of the football we all watch is at club level, and despite the apparent passion expressed by fans of either side, the differences between rival teams are generally contrived and meaningless. Domestic clubs have not been made up of local players since the 1880s when Preston North End scandalized the world of sport by fielding players from Preston's south end.

But international football is different; it is about our collective identity. Of course, our nationality probably shouldn't be at the forefront of our consciousness on a daily basis; there's probably something dodgy about your politics if it is. Sovereign states simply happen to be the way that the world is divided up and so global sport uses these same categories to allocate the teams. Mark once suggested organizing an international tournament based on signs of the zodiac. That would have made for a different sort of World Cup, when Ramos and Ribéry and Ronaldinho all played in the same team because they shared the same star sign.

'You join us here at this top-of-the-table clash in the Fire Signs group, a historic grudge match between the proud Leos and the intemperate Aries team. Russell – tough game to call?'

'Very hard to predict what will happen, Barry. Aries can expect health matters to come to the fore, whereas Leo will find work issues resolving themselves, and friends becoming important later on . . .'

We cheer for England in the football, Team GB in the Olympics and Europe in the Ryder Cup. In international rugby there is even the concept of supporting your own hemisphere. 'Yeah, I'm Northern Hemisphere, through and through me, I was born North of the Equator and dead proud of it . . .'

But of course it is not random, it does have meaning, you could not do a Wimbledon with England, relocate them to Germany and rename them *Borussia Englanders*. A shared language, culture and traditions make us feel too deep a bond. This can be harnessed as a force for good or bad, and at times I worry about the political dangers of getting tens of thousands of Englishmen into one football stadium to sing and chant about their love for their country. But football's got to be better than war – even the way the Uruguayans play it.

My mind had clearly wandered from the action on the pitch. I was watching but I had fallen into that trance-like state that means that the two teams had worn each other into a stalemate. A draw might not be enough to see us through; we would be dependent on the other result in this group. A win and we were through, defeat and we were out. 'Greece are a goal down' went the rumour – 'this might be enough.'

But from nowhere a sloppy cross-field pass was intercepted and a Polish shirt was through on goal, Luke Shaw chasing him. No! We could all see it coming; Shaw brought him down when he was the last man; penalty to Poland in the final minute, and Shaw sent off. One minute of play remaining, and all Poland have to do is score a penalty to prevent England from progressing in the European Championship.

Sure enough, the penalty did result in a goal, though not quite in the way that anyone had expected. Poland's top goal scorer carefully placed the ball on the spot. He looked up to see the English keeper poised on his line, jumping up and down in anticipation. And then he ran up and kicked the ball with all his might.

And almost in the same instant the joyful sight of the ball bouncing off the crossbar, eighty thousand people exhaling instead of drawing breath; this gift of a goal had been thrown away and the penalty was missed. So hard had he struck the ball that it bounced back in a huge loop over the heads of all the Poland players who had been rushing into the box for any rebound as it sailed towards the halfway line. Here England's Raheem Sterling had been waiting probably every game of his long career, for this incredibly unlikely possibility. Straight from a Poland penalty, Sterling was suddenly one on one with the Polish keeper. He dribbled, he swerved, he sent the keeper the wrong way, he tapped it in: 3-2!

It all happened so fast, we were still on our feet celebrating the missed penalty but now our elation had to go up a whole extra level and we had started too high, we hadn't given ourselves enough room to be this much happier. In the course of about eight seconds we had gone from almost certainly being out of the European Championship to definitely going through.

'Bloody hell; football!' the bloke beside Tom said to me, and we laughed and shook our heads in joyous disbelief. It was a goal that would be endlessly replayed on YouTube, a goal that would still be talked about in decades to come and Tom would be able to say, 'Yeah, I was there; that was my first ever international.'

'England did fantastically, didn't they, Tom?'

He corrected me on my grammar. 'It's *done fantastic*, Dad.' I had no idea he listened to so many football pundits.

After the match I thought I might impress him with a peek inside the press suite, but of course that was the one time my swipe card was getting no response at the electronic doors, and since it was too packed and chaotic to go round via reception, we allowed ourselves to be swept along with the throng of still buzzing fans heading towards the exits. I decided that this was actually the better experience; my fellow journalists would have been the only people in the entire stadium who remained emotionally detached from what had happened, it was best Tom didn't witness the blithe scepticism of his father's profession just yet.

When I finally dropped him at his mum's, he was still brimming with excitement at the match he had been privileged to witness. He gabbled his highlights and Suzanne smiled and you could see the love in her eyes and the happiness she felt for him and perhaps even some latent gratitude for the man-child who was his father. He described the goals 'in order of amazing-ness', and how anyway Poland deserved to lose because they were 'rabbit murderers' and Suzanne kept looking at me as if to say, 'Has he been drinking?' He was so thrilled by it, but most of all by the revelation that he had been part of the crowd that had turned it round – that England would never have won without us. I had only wanted to make him feel what I felt, to experience the pleasure I got from the game, but now like me, Tom was completely obsessed with England.

It would make it all the harder when I became con-flicted about going public with my suspicions. Because the drug of football was no longer strong enough to mollify me; now even the most perfect England game I'd ever seen couldn't lull me into thinking all was well with the world. And as if to confirm my suspicions, the next morning I got a curt but formal letter from the Football Association. It turned out there hadn't been a fault with my electronic swipe card; the problem was with me. My Wembley press pass had been rescinded. No reason was given.

What position would Jesus have played in?

White Shirts v Red Shirts, Five-a-side Kick-about

Somerstown Sports Centre – 21 February 2021

Urgent shouts for the ball echo around the sports hall, as trainers squeak on the wooden floor. I make a discreet move down the right as our keeper rolls the ball out to Peter in his vintage Spurs shirt. Peter cheekily bounces the ball off the wall at the perfect angle to beat Colin, and then lays it off to the centre circle where Jack has timed his run well. A quick one-two with Gary, suddenly Jack is on the left of the semicircle, and puts a perfect cross right to my feet just as I lose my marker and accelerate to power in a perfectly worked goal. Except somehow the ball pings off the top of my wrong foot and goes way over the bar from one yard out. Oh, and I manage to fall over at the same time.

'GET IT ON TARGET!!!' shouts Bryan at me.

Oh, was *that* what I was supposed to do? Thank you so much for that advice, Bryan, I thought I was actually *supposed* to launch the ball vertically off my laces and up into the rafters. That's why I just did that on purpose, obviously.

'Come on, Whites! Let's make these chances count!' shouts another teammate behind me, equally helpful on the advice front.

I had played in this five-a-side game for nearly twenty years, and though it was only supposed to be a casual kick-about, this weekly fixture was really, really important to me. Sometimes I'd be invited out to some important social event, and I would always say, 'Oh, I would have loved to – but I can't make it I'm afraid, I'm already doing something that night I can't miss.' And inside I was thinking, 'Please don't ask me what it is', because the truth never went down very well.

We played indoors at a leisure centre on a polished wooden floor with a soft five-a-side ball, and mismatched shirts and an increasing preponderance of knee-braces and supports and bandages for whichever joint or ligament was taking longer to heal than last time. Sometimes it was five-a-side, sometimes it was seven against eight; the teams were divided up from whoever turned up each week. Thankfully the sides were picked discreetly by one or two people balancing them up at the beginning; we didn't put everyone through the playground trauma of lining them up against the wall and taking turns to announce the most worthwhile human beings. That is a brutal ordeal that our society reserves exclusively for impressionable young children. All that was expected of us was that we brought one white shirt (England, Spurs, Fulham, Leeds, Real Madrid, Grubby Primark Vest) and one red shirt (England away, Manchester United, Liverpool, Arsenal, Spain, Che Guevara). The Sunderland fan always complained that we wouldn't let him wear his club shirt; 'But it's obviously red!' he would moan. 'Yeah, with white stripes, it's too confusing . . .'

I came to understand that every week, while Whites played Reds, and the score swung this way and that, another more meaningful contest was taking place. The eternal battle of *Competitiveness* versus *Sportsmanship*. You cannot have a good game without the players on the pitch trying hard and being determined to win. But you cannot have a good game if they want to win at the expense of everything else; the rules, the camaraderie and the spirit of the sport. Some weeks, a few players mucked around or couldn't be bothered to try very hard and I left the match feeling vaguely disappointed. Other weeks, the game got too fractious or over-physical and the evening was spoiled for the opposite reason. It was a special night when the yin and yang of 'Trying Really Hard' and 'Playing Really Fairly' were in perfect harmony.

In this particular game Sportsmanship went a couple behind before we even kicked off when Bryan argued about the balance of the teams and tried to get some of the best players switched to his side. (Basically the five-a-side equivalent of saying, 'We'll have Messi, Xavi, Bale; you have Eric Pickles.') Then he didn't own up to an obvious handball, but Jack put the ball down for a free kick anyway. Bryan petulantly asserted that this act was the first handball; Competitiveness ran in and kicked the ball when it was the other side's free kick, and it seemed as if tonight was going to be a very one-sided contest. Sportsmanship briefly looked like it had got one back when the ball flew up to hit Jack's hand and he immediately owned up to give a free kick to the other side, but he was actually making a point to get back at Bryan, so it didn't count.

But Sportsmanship rallied, a brilliant team goal was applauded by the opposition, inspiring both sides to a period of unselfish passing football. Competitiveness put in a positive spell as well, with players running back to cover, working hard all across the pitch. Then a disputed goal was given after a couple of the defending players confirmed that they had seen it cross the line, and Sportsmanship drew level. And with the actual score at 10-10, I realized that tonight was a truly great match. Sometimes in those games I caught myself and thought 'I *really* love this . . .'

In the changing room afterwards, congratulations were exchanged and banter dished out. 'Alfie, you're like a homeopathic footballer . . .' said Mark. 'You gave it 0.00001 per cent.' I pulled off my soaking England shirt and cast it into my bag. Underneath the three lions badge there was a little commemorative scroll that read 'UEFA Euro 2020'. I had bought the entire kit the day after that incredible victory over Poland to bring good luck for 'the rest of the tournament'. The shirt looked a little sad now, the lettering was peeling off and one of the lion's heads had disintegrated in the tumble dryer.

Perhaps I should have thrown that Euro 2020 shirt away to stop reminding myself of the disappointment. But there was some sort of masochistic penance about sticking with it. The memorable Poland game had turned out to be a high-water mark for that particular England squad. They failed to reproduce the same form and that ageing team would never play so well again. In the first knockout game of Euro 2020, they struggled to get a draw with Portugal, and then failed to take advantage in extra time when Portugal's captain got a red card. It was never very clear what he was sent off for. 'An offensive haircut' was Mark's suggestion. Inevitably it went to penalties. 'One Englishman always misses a penalty,' Mark had said ominously. In fact he was wrong. England missed their first two and even the consolation narrative of the penalty shoot-out never got going.

'Why can't they bloody practise penalties, for god's sake?' I'd shouted at the television.

'You can't practise for a penalty shoot-out,' said Mark.

'Well, you could practise kicking a ball very hard at the goal from the penalty spot. That bit you could practise.'

'You can't recreate the tension,' he said with infuriating certainty.

'THAT IS SUCH A STUPID BLOODY ARGUMENT!' I snapped. 'Do you think in World War Two they said, "Well, you can't recreate the tension of invading Normandy, so there's no point in trying out your guns before fucking D-Day"?'

'I don't think Churchill would have used the F word. Certainly not on the BBC Home Service.'

Perhaps it isn't lack of practice, perhaps there is something in our national character that makes us lose penalty shoot-outs. Even in our regular five-a-side game you learnt something about character. No matter what level the game is played at, I came to realize that we each come with our own natural position on a football pitch. It's something we're born with, like blue eyes or brown hair; hidden deep within our DNA is a gene that decides whether we are best suited to midfield or centre back or playing in goal. Sean was a defender; he blocked shots, he stifled attacks; he never made space, he always closed it down. Whenever he strayed upfield, he looked lost and ineffective, and though he could pass a ball creatively from the back, any shot would fly wide or over. He was simply meant to be a defender. Mark was a midfielder; he read the game, he ran back and covered, he was at the centre of all the creativity. But do a quick one-two with him around the box, and he'd never make that final run that might have given him an easy tap-in; there was no predatory instinct; instead he was back at the top of the D shouting for me to pass back so he could create a chance for *someone else* to score all over again.

Presumably this applies to all other sports as well; if I'd been born in the United States, I guess I'd be best suited to one particular position in American football. 'The One Who Runs Into All The Other Players', maybe? Or perhaps 'The Other One Who Runs Into All The Other Players'? Every figure in history who existed before Association Football was even invented must have had a position. I raised this notion at our weekly post-match curry.

'Vlad the Impaler?'

'Attacker, surely?'

'And probably quite a dirty player, like, Chopper Harris level . . .'

'And you don't want to think about his goal celebration with the corner flag.'

'OK, what position would Jesus have played in?' I asked.

'Up front – as the star striker,' said Mark. *'And it's another hat-trick for the Son, the Father and the Holy Ghost!'*

'Or goalkeeper perhaps?' suggested someone else. 'Saving goals and souls with his arms outstretched in the posture that he would very much make his own.'

We agreed that this must have been why there were twelve disciples; it's the perfect number for a football team, given that there's always one bloke with a hangover who fails to turn up. Peter the rock at the back, Matthew, Mark, Luke and John making up a four-man midfield, and Judas taking bribes to throw the match at the last minute.

Men need some sort of external framework to give them a reason to meet up. With the Disciples it was this new religion. With us, it was five-a-side football.

Players had come and gone down the years, but a hard core of us had grown middle-aged together, still meeting up every week as we'd settled down, had kids, got divorced or changed careers. But although I saw the same blokes week in, week out, we still knew very little about each other. I'd split up with Suzanne over a decade earlier, I had fathered her child, yet I don't think I had ever discussed any of that with any of them. In fact this typically male lack of communication was one of the things Suzanne used to find so weird about my football friends, if we ever happened to bump into one of them at some party or cinema queue.

'You never told me about Geoff. That's so interesting about him setting up a literacy charity for ex-offenders . . .'

'Has he?'

'Yes! I was talking to him about it when you were getting the drinks. Fancy the Home Office cutting his grant.'

'Oh dear, has it?'

'How can you not even know the basics about someone you have seen every week for years?'

'I do know the basics! Geoff; goal hanger, wears a Barnsley shirt, doesn't take his turn in goal.'

I'd eaten a post-match curry with these blokes every single week since my early twenties. By that token I have had more meals out with Colin the civil servant than I had with Suzanne during our entire six years together. But because this was not a group of like-minded friends acquired in the usual way, it was all the more interesting to be challenged by people with completely different values and politics.

'How can you be a socialist, Alfie, if you love football?' said Colin, a die-hard Tory who always goaded me about working for a Labour-supporting newspaper.

'What are you talking about – football is socialism in practice! The team with the plan, that cooperates, that works for one another, that will always be the team that wins.'

'So how come no socialist country ever won the World Cup?'

'That doesn't prove anything – the United States has never won it either; at least the Soviet Union were European Champions.'

'All sport is inherently capitalist. It is about competing against one another; who is strongest, fastest, most determined. A socialist football team would have Stephen Hawking up front because it would be wrong to discriminate against the disabled.'

'No – *from each according to their ability*; we would make Stephen Hawking manager, because his brilliant analysis would make us unbeatable.'

'Rubbish team-talk at half-time though,' added Mark unhelpfully. 'No passion in it.'

'Your right wing team would lose, Colin, because it would be a collection of individuals playing for themselves, not for the team.'

'Socialists have no real understanding of competitive sport. All that football money New Labour spent in their first term, and all for nothing.'

'What money?' I said, realizing he might know something I didn't.

'The billion that was set aside under Blair for "Future Football" or whatever. By the time the Iraq War came along, the money had completely dried up, and what have we got to show for it? A top division full of foreigners.'

'Steady, Colin,' said Mark. 'We're in an Indian restaurant. Don't go all UKIP on us.'

The revelation hit me like a thunderbolt. That was the source of funding for Operation Early Doors! All this time I had been wondering how a billion might have been secretly syphoned off from other government departments, while the obvious truth had been staring me in the face. They had cunningly funded their secret plan for the future of football using the money from Future Football. I never thought of looking there.

I spent long hours at Companies House, sifting through financial records and putting in further requests for every related corporation or charity I could think of. Looking through Treasury spreadsheets and Budget Committee reports, I located the enormous spike of investment in the sport between 1998 and 2002. But after many hours staring at these complex balance sheets and audits, I realized that something didn't feel right about all of this. They were like no other football accounts I had ever seen. *None of it was missing!* There were no excessive agents' commissions, no bungs or backhanders, no cash had been creamed off in lieu of 'introduction fees' or 'sundry expenses' – it was all accounted for and in order. There was something deeply suspect about the footballing types at Future Football. *They weren't corrupt.*

Most of the billion pounds had gone into the FA's specially built St George's Park National Football Centre in Staffordshire. This was the brand-new training HQ for the England national team, featuring state-of-the-art facilities, extensive accommodation, and it turned out, extremely tight security. But why did the 'Sports Science Block' cost more than the Chelsea first team? How big a science research department do you need to work out that football players should lay off the kebabs and lager? And who was the mysterious 'RW' who seemed to be in charge of this huge Sports Science budget? Ruby Wax? Ronnie Wood? Rebekah Wade?

I travelled to the local newspaper library at Boston Spa in the hope of researching the early years of the mysterious Commonwealth champions. Every professional footballer has a few old pictures of them in the front row of some junior school team, having won a local cup competition or the Under 11s league. But not these players. I painstakingly searched through the microfilms of the relevant regional newspapers but found nothing. Not one player on my list had ever turned out for a local boys' team or been mentioned in a match report. It was too consistent to be a coincidence. I tried variations of their names, I searched local papers that had long since closed down, I scanned the pictures of other teams hoping to recognize one of them, all without success. The media blackout had sounded reasonable when Greg Dyke had fobbed me off with it, but not now that it dated right back to their infancy. Where had they developed their incredible talents? Was it possible that these players had all been trained from birth behind the high-security walls of the St George's Park National Football Centre in Staffordshire?

Even before I had become aware that the FA were hiding something I had been frustrated about how little of the inside of the St George's Park Centre journalists had been allowed to see. Now I made a choice as foolish as aiming for that open goal with my left foot. I made a formal request to the FA to tour the whole building and see behind the locked doors previously denied to journalists. I said I was writing a piece on 'Future Football', explaining to football fans and taxpayers how exactly their billion pounds had been spent. I sent copies of the letter to Greg Dyke and Tony Blair.

Two days later I was in a police cell.

'No easy games at this level . . .'

Vatican City v England – World Cup Qualifier

Stadio Olimpico, Rome – 4 October 2021

In normal circumstances a mid-season clash between two amateur Essex clubs would not have grabbed my attention. However, sitting in a windowless police interview room, being shouted at and threatened with years of imprisonment as they asked me how I went about fixing this match; well, it was hard not to be curious about the result.

'Seven all, Alfie! Seven all! Does that not strike you as an unusual result?'

'Yes, but what's that got to do with me?' I stammered.

'Don't play the innocent with me, scum!' The hard-man detective crumpled a paper cup. 'Now we can do this the easy way . . . or we can do this the hard way . . .'

I can report that ITV police dramas are very accurate in the way they portray interviews of criminal suspects. Real-life officers obviously watch these gritty cop shows and imagine this is how they're supposed to behave. So they sat me in a stuffy little room, they banged the table in front of me, they paced around behind me, they told me I was 'a prize mug to take the rap for Mr Big'; all these clichés were faithfully recreated during my long day in a police station, as life imitated bad art and I felt utterly bewildered as to how this misunderstanding could have come about.

I didn't disagree that the result of that not-very-crucial clash between Billericay United v Romford Albion in the fourth round of the Pritt-Stick Southern Amateur Vase looked a little bit suspicious. Not merely because 7-7 was a ridiculous scoreline, but because this match had attracted more international bets than other matches that day involving Barcelona, Manchester United, Bayern Munich and AC Milan put together. Including, it would seem, a £1,000 bet on this exact result placed in my name.

'I never bet on football. If I did I'd be bankrupt from betting on England wins. It must be a computer error, or someone else with my name.'

'Do you ever stop to think about your victims, eh?' snarled the senior copper. 'Did you ever think about the suffering your crimes cause?'

The younger policeman looked a little worried about where his colleague might be going with this. Was he going to try and paint a pitiful picture of the weeping chief executive of an online betting giant as he contacted their fraud insurance brokers?

'Who are you working with, you filthy parasite? We want names; there's no place for greed and corruption in football.'

Again, the younger policeman looked less convinced.

Mark came to collect me from the police station late that night, offering my prized collection of Sainsbury's 1998 World Cup coins as bail, which did not even get a half-smile from the desk sergeant. He thought the whole episode was hilarious. 'It's obviously not you,' said Mark. 'Alfie Baker and organized crime? Do me a favour, *disorganized* crime maybe . . . "Oh no, I've just realized the getaway car's still outside the pub where I left it two nights ago . . ."'

I had been the victim of identity fraud before, but this was far more serious. Someone had used my name and address to open a fake bank account for online gambling on fixed matches. The police had me in for questioning three more times after that, and although it never came to anything the affair precipitated an Orwellian sequence of repeated petty harassments, 'random' car checks, rejected credit cards and an automated letter from the defrauded gambling company congratulating me on my winnings and offering me a free £5 bet.

A paranoid person might imagine that the whole episode was a warning to a nosy journalist to back off. And the shameful thing is that it worked. I never pursued my plan to try and get inside the St George's Park National Football Centre by more underhand means, and every time I thought about doorstepping a retired New Labour cabinet minister, I imagined getting duffed up as some burly bodyguard dived in and tried to pull John Prescott off me.

Instead I resolved to concentrate on the job I was supposed to be doing: following the Three Lions through their World Cup qualifying campaign – although 'lions' was probably a bit generous. Lions like that boss-eyed one in *Daktari*, maybe. These ageing veterans had looked so promising back when they'd first broken into the England squad. Once upon a time, the likes of Sturridge, Sterling and Welbeck had been exciting young prospects who gave us great hope for the future; now they looked tired and old as they made extremely hard work of qualifying for Qatar 2022. Still the England manager ignored calls to select some of the brilliant youngsters who'd become Commonwealth champions, even when it looked touch and go that England would even qualify. Fortunately the last game in their group was against joke opposition, and so their progression to the finals was a foregone conclusion.

'There are no easy games at this level . . .' the England manager said at the press conference before the game.

'With all due respect,' said one of the journalists, 'there is *one* easy game at this level, and it is against Vatican City. They are all amateurs; for Christ's sake, the Pope nearly got in the team! San Marino beat them seven-nil; surely this is the *one* elusive easy game at this level . . .'

Vatican City had made the decision to join UEFA and field a national team in the hope of improving tourism and international awareness of the tiny city-state. They were one of a number of countries or dependent territories around this time that thought they could follow San Marino and Gibraltar and raise their national profile by having their names read out alongside humiliating football results.

Vatican City was the smallest independent country in the world and did not even have a single football pitch within its 'borders'. Disappointingly, they were not managed by the Pontiff himself, although His Holiness was present for one or two of their matches and became quite animated during the games. He might have got reprimanded by the stewards for His language, if his language had not been Latin. *'Arbiter!'* he would scream. *'Caeci estis aut quid?'** But they were the joke team of the World Cup qualifiers; no wins, no

---

*Latin scholars explained that the Pope was also shouting 'Who is the man, who, having been born out of wedlock, is now wearing black?'

draws; goals for, zero, goals against, seventy-three. And as luck would have it, they were the last hurdle England had to overcome on their way to Qatar 2022. As match-fixing accusations went, a high-scoring England victory seemed to have been prearranged.

'We will be showing Vatican City as much respect as if we were playing Germany,' said the England manager.

'Why?'

'I'm sorry?'

'Why will you be showing them as much respect as Germany, when they are clearly nowhere near as good?'

'They have some very useful players,' continued the manager, to the groans of the assembled press pack.

'Yes, useful if you need a guided tour of St Peter's Basilica. The last time any of them scored was before they took their vows of celibacy.'

It should never have come to this. How could it be that England needed to beat Vatican City to be sure of qualifying for the Qatar World Cup in 2022? The national team had got off to a disastrous start in Group B with no points from their trip to Slovenia (not least because half of the England fans flew to Slovakia by mistake). Defeats against Sweden and Turkey along the way left England needing nothing less than three points from their final group game, against the worst national side in the world.

But surely, everyone agreed, that was a mere for-
mality. Vatican City were all amateurs; a team made
up of priests and church wardens; 'Vatican City Don't
Have a Prayer!' declared the back page of the *Sun*. My
own paper wouldn't even pay to send me to cover the
match. Yet there was an air of nervous anticipation as
I joined my friends in the pub an hour before kick-off.
The place was packed out with football fans reserving
their places and lining up pints so they wouldn't lose
their seats with a trip to the bar. Mark had brought his
girlfriend Jenny, who hated football.

'Why does every single screen in the pub have to be
set to the game?' she kept saying. 'It's Penguin Night
over on Animal Planet; can you ask if one of the screens
can be turned over to that?'

At that moment the barman turned up the volume
so loud that her pleas were drowned out, as we settled
in for the pre-match build-up.

'And you join us here in Rome for this vital World
Cup qualifier – England versus Vatican City in which
this very experienced England team take on the pious
part-timers from the Papal State. There's their big
goalkeeper, Cardinal Mario Mancini; most days he's
taking confession, but its goal kicks he'll be taking
today!'

'And that winger of theirs is a useful little player –
Perone, a priest by trade. Normally he is delivering

sermons, but its crosses into the box he will be delivering today . . .'

'And there's their captain, Costa – he is actually under investigation for abusing choirboys – but it's the England defence he hopes to interfere with today . . .'

The co-presenter's microphone seemed to go quiet after that, and only one commentator was heard for the rest of the match.

'Excuse me, would it be possible to have one screen switched to Animal Planet?' continued Jenny. 'Not everybody here wants to watch the football,' she said as a deafening cheer went up for the start of the game.

England were playing in red shirts, with Vatican City in white and gold, rather than the purple cassocks we'd all been hoping for. England started at a leisurely pace, keeping possession, passing the ball backwards before finally tapping it back towards their own keeper for an early touch. It's often a good idea to let the keeper get a kick of the ball so that his first contact is not under pressure, even if it's only ten seconds into the game. But not, it should be said, if the goalie is still sorting out his towel and water bottle at the side of the net. In this situation it is a *very bad idea* to pass the ball back towards the gaping goalmouth.

The pub fell into a stunned silence, apart from one delirious Italian-looking bloke in a dog collar who shouted 'Goal!' and then realized that a hundred

English lads full of lager were looking at him with total disgust, at which point he sat down quietly.

So the England goalkeeper did get an early touch of the ball when he was not under any pressure. This was because he was picking the ball out of the back of the net as Vatican City celebrated an unlikely first minute lead without having yet had a kick of the ball.

'Can we switch channel now?'

'Jenny – if you say that again I am going to chuck you.'

England were behind against Vatican City. It was San Marino '93 all over again. The boys in red took kick-off and timidly passed the ball about midfield, but now appeared so nervous of doing anything that stupid again, that no one dared take any chances by going forward. It only rubbed salt into the wound when a few minutes later the television displayed the following statistics.

	Vatican City	England
Goals	1	0
Shots on target	0	0
Possession	0%	100%

'I can't believe I am watching this!' said the commentator. 'England are losing to the team that are officially ranked as the worst national side in the whole world!'

This is how amateur Vatican City were. You know that moment when the cameraman picks out a couple of face-painted fans in the stands and they spot themselves on the giant screen, and go mad with excitement, waving in the wrong direction and excitedly nudging their friends that they are on the screen. Well, the Vatican City *players* did that as well.

The minutes dragged by and England failed to ignite. The realization that your team is playing badly creeps up on you slowly; blind faith keeps dismissing poor moments of play, refuses to see any pattern in the series of disappointing long balls or absence of creative passes. You still believe that the next incisive pass or this upcoming tackle will unleash England's true potential; like a betrayed wife in denial you refuse to see what is obvious to neutral observers. And then you realize fifteen or twenty minutes have passed and that every hopeful shift of your body in your chair has ended with disappointment; every time you mentally played that perfect one-two or internally mimed that instinctive shot, your avatar on the screen failed to cooperate and instead chose a cautious back pass or hoiked a long ball into no-man's land.

And you suddenly say out loud, 'This is rubbish!' Awareness of this fact had been suppressed in your subconscious and now you feel foolish and cheated. You'd put your trust in them and they betrayed you.

'This is the worst England team ever!' you declare in disgust. Others around you may not yet be ready to hear this – they may not have reached Stage Two of Anger; they might still be stuck at Stage One – Denial. Your negativity might seem like a betrayal of its own – a sacrilegious lack of faith that could actually *cause* England to play badly.

'This is rubbish!' concurred Mark. 'We can't even beat a Sunday league team – actually not a Sunday league team, they're not allowed to play on Sundays. But it's still rubbish.'

'So why are we still watching it?' said Jenny. 'There's loads of other things on . . .'

The Vatican's team of left-footers knew they had almost no chance of scoring again, and so put eleven men behind the ball and simply tried to hang on for the remaining . . . well, ninety minutes of the game. It was the only time I saw a team trying to run down the clock by taking the ball to the corner flag *during the first half*.

With half-time approaching and England desperate for a goal before the break, there was only one thing for it. It was time to deploy our secret weapon. Few things are certain in football except that when Mark went to the toilet he would miss an England goal. This was so established in the laws of science, that if England were 1-0 down with ten minutes to go, all our friends would beg him to go to the gents as the only chance left for the national side.

We looked at my flatmate and we didn't need to say anything more. He stood up, his chair scraped back and with the expectation of the whole country upon his shoulders he began the long walk to the urinals. And as he stood there staring at the graffiti on the wall, thinking about England going out of the World Cup in the most embarrassing manner possible, he suddenly heard a huge roar go up from the bar, followed by shouts of 'Yes!' and 'Come on!' and he knew that his job was done. *Match of the Day* always interviews the players and the managers after the game; they really should have talked to Mark because his timely visit to the pub urinals was the real reason that England got the equalizer.

'So, Mark, another goal at a crucial moment in the game? Talk us through the build-up to that vital piss.'

'It had been coming for a while, to be honest – I'd had several pints of lager, and missed a couple of chances to go earlier on . . .'

'And what a powerful wee it was!'

'Well, I just got sight of the urinal and let it go. Normally I'd go for straight down the middle, but I saw a gap between the chewing gum and the giant polo thing and so I aimed for that. Luckily for me it hit the target, so, yeah. Delighted.'

Everyone in the pub seemed to believe that order had now been restored to the world; that England were on their way and another couple of goals after the restart would soon allow us to relax and start looking forward to a great summer of football.

I got a text from Tom: *Great goal eh Dad?* :-) and I felt momentarily guilty that I was not watching this match at home with my ten-year-old boy. He was looking forward to this World Cup more than anything, really believing that England could win it, despite the shambles of the qualifying stages. Sharing a passion for football with Tom had taken my investment in the England team to a whole new level. He opened up when we talked about football; we had whole sentences together, back-and-forth conversations involving conjecture and analysis and shared jokes. And having a dad who wrote about the England football team increased my son's status in the playground. Each England success reflected a tiny amount of glory on to Tom, each England disappointment made him slightly less interesting to his classmates.

The England team came out for the second half looking marginally more confident and played with greater fluency and composure. But they were missing a vital component: luck. The team hit a run of bad fortune with every deflection going against them, hitting the woodwork four times in twelve minutes and failing to get a couple of marginal penalty calls.

'I've seen them given!' said the pundit on the television.

'Yes, but should it have been a penalty?'

'I've seen 'em given.'

'Yes, but that incident in particular, Ron – do you think that should have been a spot kick?'

'I've seen 'em given.'

One shot rebounded off the Vatican City post to hit the other post, and spun up into the hands of their keeper, who had been lying in the goalmouth helplessly watching it all. Luck had been left in the dressing room. Luck had gone off injured at half-time. Unlike the first half, England deserved to be winning, but weren't.

But as the second half wore on, England's promising burst of energy subsided and the Vatican City players were able to keep kicking the ball into the stands where the crowd held on for as long as they could. With ten minutes to go it became a distinct possibility that England were going to draw with Vatican City and fail to qualify for Qatar.

Einstein must have discovered that time is relative when he was watching a football match; the minutes actually do pass much more quickly if your team desperately needs to score before the final whistle. Eighty-five minutes became eighty-six minutes. Eighty-seven minutes seemed to skip one and go straight to eighty-nine. Come on, England! One more heave!

Then England get a corner. Our goalkeeper comes up to the other end. Against Vatican Bloody City! But about three of their defenders rush to mark him, leaving the England strikers free to receive the cross. Which is when the England captain chooses to take a short corner.

'NO!!!' screams the whole pub in unison.

'The fucking final whistle is about to blow, you twats!' I hear myself shout, as I rise to my feet. 'You have the chance for a direct cross into the goalmouth, but instead you fanny about down by the touchline, risking the chance of making *no cross at all*, why the fuck would you choose to take a short corner?'

Strangers look around and nod in agreement with the angry fan. But from the improved angle, the cross goes in, the Vatican defence still looks confused, players are crashing into one another, a leg is stuck out and the ball heads towards the line . . . and . . .

'YES!'

Such is the eruption of released tension in the pub that I don't actually see the moment. Everyone is hugging one another as we watch the action replay and see the cross come in as a couple of Vatican City players fall over and the ball bounces off the knee of one of them and into the net. The England players are celebrating. We are jumping up and down in the pub, beer is spilling, a hundred England shirts are hugging one another.

'Didn't I just say he ought to take a short corner?'

A moment of uncertainty. The Vatican players indicate that the linesman is gesturing towards the referee. But it was definitely a goal; we saw the replay, there was no offside, no foul, and the ball definitely crossed the line; we all saw England get that crucial goal and win the game. The referee waves the England players away from the linesman as they confer. The linesman looks like a bit of a maverick, the sort of character who craves attention, good or bad.

'No goal!' says the commentator. 'England have been robbed!'

The referee indicates that a shirt was tugged, but the replay clearly shows a Vatican defender pulling over one of his own teammates; the linesman has got it completely wrong. Now the frustration is too much and the players are jostling the referee. A yellow card is shown and then another one. A glass is smashed in the pub. Hands are covering faces; we can't believe what has just happened. Maybe they will quickly get another goal to ensure justice is done? But aware that he has lost control of the game, the referee quickly blows the final whistle, without allowing for the stoppage that this controversy has caused, and an extra injustice is heaped upon the England camp. The final score is 1-1. England finish third in their group and fail to qualify.

At which point Jenny took her headphones out of her ears and said, 'Finally! Can we watch the other channel now?'

'Jenny. I'm coming round tomorrow to collect my stuff,' said Mark. 'And then I will never see you again.'

England would not be going to the 2022 World Cup in Qatar. Mark and I had spent twenty quid on beer but now felt stone-cold sober. I got a text message from Suzanne: *Tom in tears*. It made me feel that somehow the linesman's decision had been my fault.

I wandered home doing up my jacket to cover my England shirt. The disappointment left me hollow and angry. Tom and I had been going to share this World Cup together; by the time of the next World Cup he would probably be too old to be bothered – a teenager more interested in music or fashion, leaving me as the sad dad to watch the games alone.

And I realized that with England out of the Qatar World Cup, they might bring forward the redundancies on the sports pages. Did that linesman put me out of a job, along with the England manager? Was this it for football and me? I got home and felt much too old to be returning to a barely furnished, smelly lads' flat. I looked at my elaborate noticeboard. A secret conspiracy to ensure England won the World Cup? We couldn't even bloody qualify! I ripped down all the photos and the Post-it notes, I tore up the pictures of the stars of old. That was all history; it was never going to happen again, get over it, Alfie! I went to bed. And then put the pillow over my ear to try and block out Mark, shouting at the TV as he watched the England highlights being repeated over on ITV2.

What is the point of the shot-put?

Bishops Common – 26 March 2022

When someone suffers a bereavement, they often deliberately busy themselves with digging the garden or clearing out the cellar to try and avoid dwelling upon their loss. So it was with the death of my relationship with football. This Saturday, I would not be wasting my free time watching my team draw 0-0 at home, I would just give the flat a thorough spring clean while the radio kept me company in the background. Not Radio 5 Live, obviously. On Radio 4 there was an hour-long play tackling a difficult but important social issue.

Because it was over. Football had kept promising me so much, but finally the scales had dropped from my eyes as I realized that this relationship had been suffocating me all these years. England's humiliating and unjust exit from the World Cup was the final straw.

I was not going to let myself fall for it again. I emailed my publishers and told them I would not be finishing my history of the England football team and that I would return their small advance 'early doors'. I made a conscious decision to abandon my investigation as well. The noticeboard came down; I hid away the files and put stupid thoughts of conspiracies and cover-ups out of my head. I had other interests now, I had better ways to spend my time; look at me, Football; I'm listening to a radio drama!

To be honest, the play was a bit rubbish. I twiddled the dial on the radio, and for a split second caught the high-octane live commentary from a Premiership football match. It was like the waft of a passing cigarette under the nose of an ex-smoker. But I was strong, I was certain; and I continued along the dial until I found an easy-listening station playing mellow hits of yesteryear.

'Mmm . . . that was the Carpenters with "Rainy Days and Mondays",' crooned the DJ. 'And it may not be a Monday, but it's certainly a bit of a rainy day in most places, so I hope your loved ones took their raincoats if they've gone to any of the football matches being played today. Latest scores from around the grounds coming up after this, from Dusty Springfield . . .'

'For god's sake! Some of us may not be interested in the football!' I said out loud to the radio. 'Honestly, everywhere you turn, football, football, football!' And

I switched off the radio before Dusty Springfield had had the chance to change the lyrics of 'I Just Don't Know What to Do with Myself' to 'I Know, I'll Get Sky Sports and Start Supporting Stoke'.

I had all this spare time; it was so liberating, I was free to read novels, visit art galleries, go for long walks . . . Obviously I never did get round to doing any of these things, but it was good to know I was free to do so, should the mood strike me. And then it was Sunday afternoon and I found myself sitting in a chair in the kitchen, not quite sure what to do with myself. I decided to give some other sports a try. I had always presumed that those non-subscription sports channels were free because they featured events that almost nobody wanted to watch. But you have to give these things a go. 'Live athletics from Helsinki' . . . I settled in with an open-minded expression of positive concentration.

This is the narrative of the long jump. 'Here comes the long jumper. He's running up to the sandpit . . . And he's jumped a long way! Not quite as far as he had hoped, but it is still a very long jump from the long jumper. So that's him done for the day.'

It just didn't seem to have the ebb and flow of an extended team sport involving a ball; the hour and a half of alternating leads, the theatre, the characters, the shifting spirit and morale of a team, the near miss or unlikely goal that twisted the plot this way and that as the clocked ticked down. Ditto the discus; you spin around with a special disc trying not to fall over. You chuck it as far as you can. The winner is whoever chucked it furthest.

'And then what?'

'No, that really is it.'

If football had been designed by the people who came up with athletics it would go like this: 'And the German captain steps up to kick the ball . . . And he has kicked it a very long way! That's a remarkable 122.3 metres . . . But will that be enough to win the World Cup? And here comes the England captain; oh and he slipped as he took his kick, and they are sticking the little flag in at 83.5 metres; a disappointing kick there from England; so it's all over, the German team are celebrating another World Cup win, as the fans start to head for the exits.'

I remember how after the London Olympics everyone had briefly raved about athletics, claiming how the modest heroics of Team GB put the pampered Premiership stars to shame. But of course any sport would develop villains and controversy if we obsessed over it in the way we did with our most popular sport. The Summer Olympics was a holiday romance; football is the marriage.

So athletics never really did it for me. I could just

about see the notion of sport in a running race; at least that had a beginning, a middle and an end. But the shot-put? Who came up with that one? Did it emerge from the history of warcraft in the way that the javelin evolved from spear throwing? When the cannon was bust, did they wonder if the big fat bloke might be able to simply throw the cannonball at the enemy? 'Oh dear me, that's nowhere near. Never mind, we'll make it a Track and Field event instead.'

As part of my traumatic divorce from football, I decided that I actually wanted to be the member of staff that Hugo had let go of at the end of the year. I was too old to be travelling all over the country writing match reports and chasing transfer rumours about people half my age. Simply resigning my job would have left me seriously out of pocket – I needed to get the sack. I needed him to actually read the sports pages for once and think, 'Whoa, we can't have this in the paper' and then make his easy decision about who would be getting that redundancy package. One of my jobs was to tweak the wording of the celebrity guest who would be making that weekend's Premiership predictions. Well, I say 'tweak'; in fact I rewrote it completely.

So the forecast of Dame Shirley Williams, former Education Minister and leader of the Liberal Democrats in the House of Lords, read as follows: *Chelsea v West Ham United; AWAY WIN. Chelsea scum gonna get dems headz kicked in by ICF boyz*, predicted Dame Shirley. *Shed End wankerz is batty boyz, true – Green St Massive gonna smash you up proper.* I thought that ought to do the trick. The subeditor corrected all the spellings, and then the item got cut to make way for a Stairlift advert. My P45 and six months' wages were nowhere to be seen.

I was given the copy of the 'You Are the Ref' feature. Although this popular long-running cartoon was ostensibly written by a Premiership referee, in reality one of our journalists took notes down the phone and then wrote out the actual text. The scenario this particular week was something like: 'It is a highly charged local derby. A striker through on goal has only the keeper to beat, but he is brought down by an opposing defender. You are about to send him off when you notice the linesman flagging for offside. What should you do?' I started to write the usual pompous verbiage: 'Assess the situation quickly and deal with these offences in the order that they occurred . . .' when I broke off and decided I would write what a ref would actually do. 'Attempt an annoying and exaggerated phoney laugh, and run away backwards. Follow this up with an over-emphatic "No!" while shaking your head far more than is natural. Also, be a bald twat.' For the other two scenarios, I just repeated the final sentence: 'Be a bald twat.' When this version was printed verbatim on Saturday morning the editor was apparently delighted. The particular referee featured in the illustration asked if he could buy the original to frame and put up in his toilet.

So while the England manager seem to have worked out a successful strategy for getting himself sacked, I couldn't even manage that. In any case my divorce from football could never be total. Somehow I had won custody of the kids; I was still supposed to be managing Junction Juniors every weekend. Only now I found myself irritated by their obsessive talk about football as if nothing else mattered.

'England could still qualify,' said Tom's friend Charlie, as the kids pulled on their boots to play Holy Trinity FC, a junior church team just above them at the foot of the table.

'No, Charlie, England cannot qualify,' I said sternly.

'It is still possible though. Because if—'

'NO, CHARLIE, ENGLAND CANNOT QUALIFY!' I snapped. 'Even if the teams above us lose their remaining games ten-nil, we still won't have enough points to finish first or second. England are not going to Qatar. That's it! It's over! Football is a bastard! Get used to it!'

I think I may have been a little over-emphatic, because when I finished I looked up to see there were eleven young faces staring at me open-mouthed.

Five minutes later the kids ran out on to the pitch

with Charlie taking up my son's former position in goal. While the ball pinged this way and that off a flock of boys failing to tame it somewhere near the centre circle, I wandered over to where he was making a big deal of placing his towel on the side netting as he'd seen the professionals do on the telly.

'Sorry if I cut you a bit short there, Charlie. It's just I'm really disappointed about England being knocked out before the tournament has even begun . . .'

'It's OK,' he said. 'All I was going to say was, if Turkey have to pull out of the World Cup because of the civil war, then England go through as next-best qualifiers.'

He was looking directly at me and must have registered my stunned reaction. An opposing striker was bearing down on his goal, but I didn't think to tell him to turn around or close down the angle.

'What did you say?'

'It was on the news this morning. If the religious conflict in Eastern Turkey gets any worse, they may have to pull out of the World Cup. That would let England in.'

At that exact moment the opposition scored their first goal.

'Oh my god – I'm so happy!' I shouted. 'This is the best thing that's happened, ever!'

I think the visitors scored quite a few more goals, but I spent most of the game searching the Internet on my phone. All the news about the sacking of the disgraced

England manager had rather taken my eye off the international politics pages and the growing crisis in Turkey. It was terrible. Seeing the burning buildings and the fleeing refugees sort of put it all in perspective. There we were, worrying about a meaningless football tournament, when a few thousand miles away lives were being lost, communities destroyed, homes razed to the ground. Terrible. Really terrible.

But just out of interest, I decided, it would be worth knowing what exactly the FIFA protocol was if a country pulled out of the tournament.

'Sorry I was a bit distracted today, guys. I'm presuming we lost again?'

'Six-nil,' said an unbroken yet world-weary voice at the back.

'Six-nil? Oh well, at least we're consistent. No, the reason I was on my iPhone all match was that I was reading about the terrible situation in Turkey.'

I felt this was a good opportunity to put things in perspective.

'Is it true then? Are they going to have to pull out of the World Cup?'

'Well, that's not what's important, is it? I mean football becomes a bit irrelevant when you read about a terrible war tearing a country apart like that.'

'But does that mean England get through?' said Jamie excitedly.

'Look – I know you're young and you're footy mad, but you have to think about the bigger picture here. People are getting killed. Villages are being destroyed . . .'

They did their best to look sombre and grown-up. 'Turkey is supposed to be a member of NATO. If Islamic militants do manage to overthrow the government and seize NATO bases, that could drag in the Western powers, then Russia might not stand by; it could escalate into a major conflict resulting in many thousands of deaths.'

There was a pensive silence amongst the team.

'But . . .' I continued, as I knew what they were all thinking because I was thinking it too, '. . . as far as I can work out from the FIFA website, if a team pulls out, the rules are that it is the next-best qualifier from the same group that goes through, not the best overall runner-up.'

'YES!' said Jamie, punching the air.

'That's what happened in 1992. War-torn Yugoslavia had to withdraw from the European Championship, allowing in Denmark, who were right behind them.'

I could almost see the hope welling up inside them.

'And then of course Denmark went on to win it,' I added carelessly.

'Oh yes!' said the kids, as if this was some sort of omen for England's renewed chances.

Two days later Islamic extremists won control of the Turkish capital and NATO forces bombed positions in Eastern Turkey. Full-scale war had begun. Britain's Prime Minister spoke to news reporters outside Downing Street, explaining that he'd been in constant touch with his American and European counterparts. It was clear that other NATO members favoured swift military action to reinstate the deposed pro-Western Turkish government. But the response being proposed by Her Majesty's Government was to simply monitor the situation for the time being, and to avoid over-hasty interference in the internal affairs of another country. Though the PM did add he'd be urging the United Nations to impose an immediate boycott of Turkey, banning them from all international cultural and sporting events. He never really explained how this might help.

'You'll win nothing with kids'

England v China – World Cup Group A

Khalifa Stadium, Doha – 26 November 2022

In 1870, the world's first international football match took place between England and Scotland. I wonder if a couple of England fans went to the pub afterwards and reflected on the merits of the team they had just seen.

'So tell me, who would be in your All-Time England football team?'

'What do you mean, my *All-Time* England football team? There's only ever been *one* England football team. Eleven players in eleven positions. That's it.'

'Hmm . . . you're right. This conversation's a bit of a non-starter, isn't it?'

A hundred and fifty years later, international football had evolved into the greatest circus in the world; the richest, most popular, glamorous, and indeed corrupt media and sporting extravaganza on the planet. One dodgy FIFA President was replaced with another and the circus rolled into its next venue. For a one-off tournament lasting less than a month, it was apparently worth constructing a modern Xanadu in the middle of the Arabian desert.* Qatar had been built in a hurry, possibly during a special edition of *Grand Designs*. Kevin McCloud would have explained that the sheikh was strictly limited to a budget of a billion trillion dollars but fortunately had got round the planning officers by chucking them all in prison. The specially built hotels, the stadiums, the transport infrastructure was all built just to accommodate the 2022 World Cup – it was the greatest testament I had ever seen to the global power of football. It set me wondering again; if a country was prepared to do this much merely to *host* the World Cup, how far would they be prepared to go to actually *win* it?

The Qatar World Cup was so extreme and unconventional in every way possible that England's circuitous route to qualification was barely noticed by the rest of

---

*A few years after Qatar had been awarded the 2022 World Cup, the football authorities became aware of a complication that they could never have possibly foreseen when considering the original bid. That July in Qatar is very, very hot. A protracted debate followed about air-conditioned stadiums or a May tournament, but the eventual compromise was to move the tournament to the winter even though this was the middle of the domestic season. There had been one other possible solution that Mark had helpfully suggested in a postcard to Sepp Blatter: 'Don't hold the World Cup in fucking Qatar.'

the world. There were so many bizarre stories and out-rageous attempts to bribe, cheat or mislead the football authorities that anyone playing good football was al-most an annoying distraction.

It was the first tournament in which twelve men succeeded in playing an entire half without anyone noticing. The reason that no one noticed was that Qatar were equally as rubbish with twelve men as they would have been with eleven. Their 0-8 deficit to United States at half-time included three own goals; they might have conceded fewer if they hadn't had so many of their own players on the pitch. But the Emir of Qatar had bought this World Cup and was determined to get his money's worth. He made himself centre forward and his rather nervous teenage son their goalkeeper. The fifty-three-year-old President huffed and puffed around the middle of the pitch with his big belly sticking out under his shirt, but clearly did not have much experience playing football. It was certainly the only time at a World Cup that I saw a player take a throw-in *underarm*. The final score was 17-0 to the United States, and for some American fans it was the only soccer result they ever felt fully satisfied with. Their centre forward Ziegfeld scored a record ten goals, but even if he hadn't completely dominated the game, the headline would still have been 'Ziggy played Qatar'.

And now the stakes were higher for me than I could

possibly have anticipated. Because finally the young players I had championed for years were taking centre stage. The new England manager had taken the bold step of sacking the entire squad of ageing donkeys who'd failed to beat Vatican City and to the amazement of football pundits everywhere, he had called up the next generation, the Commonwealth champions, my mysterious twenty-two! As a football fan I had wanted to punch the air when I'd heard the news; at last England were in with a decent chance of making a real impression on this tournament – finally the team I had researched and obsessed over were representing their country at the highest level.

But now every other paper was attempting to write player profiles, background stories, anecdotes and observations – nearly all of them cut and pasted from my many articles on them. 'This is the team the *Sun* are dubbing "The Miracles",' wrote Bill Butler, copying the piece in the *Mirror* where I had first dubbed them 'The Miracles'.* But my investigation had hit a brick wall, the mysterious leaks seemed to have stopped. And now that these players were under the spotlight,

---

*I got so fed up with journalists stealing all my hard-earned material on these new stars that in one article I planted one completely made-up fact purely so I could watch it being replicated in various other newspapers. The middle name of the England goalie was not really 'Janet'. Unfortunately this quickly became accepted as fact, and for years afterwards fans would chant 'Janet' every time he took up his place in the goal.

surely others would start to notice the eerie similarities between them and England stars of old, the gaps in their biographies, the excessive protection and secrecy. If I didn't get the story on them soon, someone else would steal the ball and score my goal.

My suspicion that there was something unusual about this England team was duly confirmed when they actually won their opening group game in some style. Final score, England 3 – China 0! When did we ever start a World Cup campaign without a disappointing draw? England's youngsters looked in command from start to finish and secured our best-ever start to a World Cup tournament. There had been some concern that China's rise as an economic and military power might be duplicated on the football pitch, but it seemed that having a billion men to choose from was still not an advantage.

'Well, it would take ages, wouldn't it?' said Bill in the bar afterwards.

'What are you talking about?'

'Right, everyone stand against the Great Wall of China and we'll pick sides . . .'

Bill was sceptical about my suggestion that this England team could go all the way. 'You'll win nothing with kids!' he kept repeating, as if this wasn't a tired old cliché by now. I resolved to write a follow-up piece to England's opening victory arguing why age didn't matter: *You'll Win Nothing With Kids, except the World Cup!* Back in my hotel room, I wrote my introduction and then checked my inbox. Suzanne had sent me highlights of Tom's match that she'd recorded on her phone. And so while I attempted to formulate an argument about the advantages of youth in team sports, I kept cutting back to watch my son's team being utterly thrashed because, unlike their opposition, Tom's team had not yet reached puberty.

Grim experience had taught me that only one question really matters when you are pitching two teams of boys against one another: *which side have got descended testicles.* Skills, training, tactics, teamwork . . . none of these factors count for anything as much as having a team with hairy armpits. The kids I managed were all angelic, prepubescent little Oliver Twists. But the squads we played against always seemed to be packed with gruff, muscular near-adults with bulging biceps, moustaches and quite possibly a baby or two back at home. Sometimes they wore sleeveless shirts to show off the rippling shoulders that would soon be barging our fragile eleven-year-olds off the ball. Whenever we turned up for a game and saw the other team warming up, I'd always know straight away whether we had already won or lost that game. The results had been guaranteed before we kicked off: *Unbroken Voices 0, Stubbly Adam's Apples 7; No Zits 0, Wispy Moustaches 8.*

And now I winced as I watched my son and his friends being out-muscled, out-run and out-fought in every department. Suzanne's recording was of pretty poor quality, but it wasn't as bad as the football. Even though this ordeal had occurred thousands of miles away, I still felt like somehow it was my fault. Since it was still early evening back in the UK, I shot him a quick text.

Great England result eh? Just watched bits of yr game from this a.m. Bad luck!! Not really fair, they were much bigger than u! Love Dad x

Normally Tom always replied straight away, now the delay made me a little anxious. Finally my phone beeped and the rush of excitement quickly turned to sadness.

Dad, I don't want to play 4 Junction Juniors anymore. Do u mind? Sorry. x

And I wondered if ultimately there was that much difference between me and the Emir of Qatar, who had forced his young son to continue playing in goal against some of the best strikers in the world.

Of course I don't mind. x

Even though it was only a text message, I'm sure he could tell I was lying.

That had been the thing we did together. Football

was the basis of our diplomatic relations. I thought back to all the Saturdays I had picked him up in his kit, how we walked up to the common side by side, the light percussion of his studs on the pavement. This mission gave us permission to talk about other stuff: his friends, his school, everything he was thinking. I could never just sit him down opposite me in my kitchen and ask him directly about those things; that would never work.

I never did finish my piece about the advantages of young football players. I watched the replay of the England game and eventually went down to the bar for a late-night whisky.* As I headed into the hotel lobby, I recognized a fellow countryman leaving the building. It was that scientist with the moustache who used to do TV shows about babies. When Tom was born, Suzanne had asked me if I'd been watching them, and I had to pretend I had.

'That bloke with the moustache . . .' I said to the receptionist. 'I think he's quite famous back in England.'

'Lord Winston?' he said with a polite smile.

'Oh yes, that's it!' And I headed towards the bar. Then I stopped and turned to face him again. 'RW!' I declared in amazement.

---

*Alcohol was only available to non-Qatari nationals. Which seemed a bit harsh, given the way their national team must have been feeling.

'I beg your pardon, sir?'

'RW stands for Robert Winston!'

'Er, yes it does . . .'

The receptionist seemed to find this fact less amazing than I did, as I walked away repeating it over and over again. That was the missing piece of the jigsaw! So the government's secret working party charged with guaranteeing that England won the World Cup had included the country's foremost expert on genetics and reproduction? A quick Internet search confirmed that RW was a Labour lord and an Arsenal fan, and then a slightly longer trawl through Google Images revealed photos of him with Greg Dyke and Tony Blair sitting at a football match together. But not any match: the final of the Commonwealth Games. Why would the three of them fly all the way to New Zealand just to watch some England youngsters play in the Commonwealth Games?

'RW . . .' I said out loud to myself. I felt the thrill of a detective making a key breakthrough in an impossible case. I stayed up all night, putting the pieces of this mystery back together, certain now that this team was the product of some extraordinary scientific breakthrough. The excitement followed me around; it replayed in my head like a great England victory. Only this was weirdly better – I was exhilarated about something I'd actually achieved myself. Could it really be that I was on the verge of revealing the truth behind the England team and breaking one of the great journalistic exclusives of all time? Was this the tournament when I would win the Journalism World Cup?

Chess with athletes

England v France – World Cup Group A

Thani bin Jassim Stadium, Doha – 30 November 2022

Tabloid newspapers have a habit of revisiting the default historic grudge or obvious battle between England and whichever national football team they happen to be facing. But with France . . . well, where do you start? *'Will the French be seeking revenge for their defeat in the War of the Palatine Succession?'* asked none of the tabloids. *'Thoughts of the 1418 Siege of Rouen never far below the surface when these two nations meet . . .'* In the run-up to the England v France game, the *Daily Mirror* managed an updated version of the Bayeux Tapestry with King Harold scoring a goal despite having an arrow in his eye. The *Sun* did a piece on the French injury problems purely so they could contrive a headline involving the phrase 'Frogs' Legs'. The *Guardian* asked different football experts to come up with their All-Time French XI. The pundits plumped for pretty much the same stars: Michel Platini, Zinedine

Zidane and Thierry Henry. The only surprise selection came from the Minister for Sport who had perhaps slightly misunderstood the brief. His All-Time French XI featured Napoleon, Brigitte Bardot and Asterix.

English football fans had seen too many false dawns to get over-excited by England's easy victory against China. The received wisdom was that this promising young squad were only here to get tournament experience. But win the World Cup with a bunch of twenty-two-year-olds? Never. This absolute certainty did a complete about-turn in under ninety minutes on 30 November 2022. Somewhere between England's first and fourth goal against the much-respected French team, the received wisdom went directly from 'England don't have a chance' to 'England could actually go all the way and become champions of the world'.

It wasn't just the speed of this England team that was superior, it was their tactics, their vision, and yes, their apparent experience. The young England players could really run; that was expected. But more importantly this team knew *where to run*. I was once asked by a non-fan what I loved about the game, and I explained to him that football is basically *chess with athletes*. You have different players arranged around the pitch; they each have special abilities and strengths. And as a fan you spend ninety minutes thinking, 'That one should move up there, so that one could move across there to cover, allowing that one to take up that space there . . .' But the real delight in chess with athletes comes not when they find the strength or skill to do exactly as you had been willing them to do, but when they see a possibility you had not; when they make a brilliant move that you didn't realize was available. Checkmate, final whistle; the superior tactics won.

The victory over France was the moment the nation started to believe in this World Cup team. It was the breakout game, the match that took the World Cup song to number one, the result that put sport at the top of the news instead of at the end. The French football had been slow, repetitive and unfathomable; it was just like their films.

It was particularly sweet because us Brits had always privately rather resented the French for creating FIFA and inventing the World Cup in the first place. It had not been their sport to run with. If today for example, Belgium suddenly announced it was creating the 'World Baseball Cup', the Americans might be entitled to think the Belgians were being a little presumptuous and ignore the whole thing. So it was with la *Fédération Internationale de Football Association*. In fact, it's hard not to conclude that FIFA owes its very existence to nothing more than an imaginative attempt by the French to annoy the English. And since a Frenchman had won the presidency of FIFA, the organization had continued to be as rude as possible to the English at every opportunity. Public debates between Greg Dyke and Michel Platini were like the exchanges between King Arthur and the French guard in *Monty Python and the Holy Grail*.

So it was hard to resist a little gloating at a final score that read England 5 – France 0.* England were certain to progress to the knockout stages and the players became superstars almost overnight.

I had already ascertained that this cohort was particularly hard to speak to, even before they became the World Cup squad. Now contact with them was virtually impossible. The hotel and training ground security was like nothing I'd ever seen; there were electric fences around the grounds, armed guards, infrared sensors and dogs. 'Is all of this to deter terrorists?' I asked the man at the gatehouse.

'No,' he said knowingly. 'Tabloid journalists.'

I was never going to get even close to quizzing any of the England football team or staff, but there was one figure in my vague conspiracy theory who could not be

---

*Back home the French team were pelted with fruit as they stepped off the plane, but this being France at least all the fruit was locally sourced and ripened to perfection. When the Russian team were pelted with fruit, it was still in the tin.

told what to do and where to stay. And he was arriving in Doha the next day with the express intention of talking to journalists. It says something about the shifting power of celebrity that it was easier to get close to a former Prime Minister than the England World Cup squad.

Tony Blair's thin face looked far too tanned for a man with hair that grey. His forehead was now permanently lined with the frown that appeared whenever he answered difficult questions about his premiership. But now he was at the World Cup in his latest capacity as UN Global Peace and Reconciliation Envoy (one of many highly paid consultancies, this one required four meetings a year to resolve all intractable wars and injustices around the world). This press conference was part of his campaign to get FIFA backing for the idea of an Israel v Palestine friendly. The description 'friendly' was being used in its loosest sense here; when the two associations said they might consider the idea, angry mobs attacked both headquarters and burned them to the ground. Never one to be discouraged by strident opposition, Blair continued to promote this pet project, arguing that as part of the process of Israel and Palestine learning to accept one another, playing a game of international football might be an invaluable step. You had to admire his high ideals. And the day before a resurgent England team played in the World Cup finals seemed as good a time as any to fly out to the finals to talk about it.

In fact his visit was booked long before England were even expected to be at this tournament and the former Prime Minister certainly would not have chosen this moment to schedule a press conference if he had been able to predict the next big game on everyone's mind. The final match in Group A would pitch the favourites to win the group against the team currently lying bottom. England versus Iraq.

'Mr Blair! Mr Blair!' came the first question. 'Do you think the Iraqi team might be concealing weapons of mass destruction?'

Blair did his best to affect a good-natured chuckle and reminded us that he wasn't here to talk about the England game, but about the role of sport in international diplomacy 'particularly where the problems seem intractable, as with the Palestinian situation'.

'Tony, are you going to ask the Americans to bomb the Iraqi goalmouth before England attack?'

Blair chuckled slightly less at this question and moved on to the subject of Palestine and the two-state solution.

'All right, for this pointless Arab–Jew match thing that you're proposing,' slurred Bill Butler, 'how long do you think each half should be?'

Blair did his puzzled look and said, 'Same as any match, forty-five minutes.'

'So, just long enough to prepare WMDs then?' And all the journalists fell about laughing.

Eventually Tony Blair lost patience. 'Look, I think we've been over all this enough times already. What happened, happened, and of course it would have been preferable if there'd never been any difficult choices to make, but the fact is Iraq have qualified for the World Cup and, you know, ask yourself if that would have happened if Saddam Hussein had still been in power? I'm here to promote peace between Israel and Palestine, so could we perhaps have a question from one of those countries?'

'Palestine is not a country,' snapped an Israeli journalist.

'Israel is Nazi state,' said a Palestinian, perhaps being a little careless with his choice of historical extremists. Voices were raised, there was some shoving, chairs were knocked over and the security staff had to pull delegates apart as the press conference broke up in disarray.

But in amongst all of that I had managed to slip in one vaguely supportive and pertinent question which I think Blair had appreciated, and as he left with his minders, I handed the former Prime Minister my card and asked if I could talk about the idea on a one-to-one basis.

That night I was fast asleep and in the middle of a dream in which my old Maths teacher was playing up front for Palestine, who were also Junction Juniors, when the referee's whistle turned into my mobile phone ringtone. I was jolted awake and saw the word 'Blocked' on the identity of the caller.

'Alfie Baker? I have Tony Blair on the line for you.'

I don't know why I leapt out of bed and stood up; it's not like it made it any more respectful, given that I was completely naked.

'Alfie, it's Tony Blair here.'

Instinctively I used my spare hand to cover myself up.

'Oh er – hello, Tony, Mr Blair.'

'Look, I was grateful that you at least seemed a bit interested in the prospect of this Palestine–Israel friendly, and a bit of coverage in the *Mirror* would be extremely helpful to us . . .'

'Oh, well, yes, no problem. Very important cause, and you never know, the Palestinians might actually win it?' I gabbled. ''Cos Jews are rubbish at sport, aren't they? I don't mean that in a racist way. They're good at everything else. I love Jewish people. And Arabs. I love all men. Though not in a gay way.'

It was probably for the best that I'd never been a panellist on *Question Time*. He patiently allowed me to finish embarrassing myself, and then he talked through the steps that were needed for FIFA to endorse this controversial fixture. When I'd calmed down, we actually talked for some time. I grew in confidence, carrying my mobile out on to my hotel balcony, where an Arab couple on the next terrace were a bit shocked to see a naked European chatting on his phone.

'Can I just ask you something else, Mr Blair?'

'Is it about Iraq?' he said wearily.

'Indirectly. You spend a lot of time having to defend stuff you did that people are negative about. But I'd like to let them know that this fantastic England team is all thanks to you.'

It's not often you hear a politician completely lost for words.

'Thanks to me?' he said after a long pause.

'I know about Future Football,' I lied. 'Some time ago I spotted the similarities between these players and their . . . shall we say, *historical influences*? This team looks unbeatable and they are only here because of you and Greg Dyke and Robert Winston. Why keep your role secret? People hear "Blair" and think "Iraq". If I broke this story, they might think "Blair – World Cup winner!"'

The dynamic of the conversation was reversed. Now he was the one mumbling and tripping over words. He muttered some vague platitude about Future Football simply being about investing at the grass roots, but he was so unconvincing that a hard-hitting satirist might have deliberately misspelt his name 'B-liar'.

'If England win the World Cup, it won't be the *former* Prime Minister welcoming the heroes at the airport. You'll be stuck somewhere else, defending your record for the millionth time. I'm going to publish the big secret about this team anyway,' I claimed. 'But if you let me have access to some documents, I can put you at the centre of the story and you'll spend the rest of your public life being cheered instead of booed.'

'What big secret?' His tone had changed. It was as if the former world leader suddenly remembered his status and that he was supposed to be in charge of this call. 'What big secret are you going to publish anyway? Do you really think I have never heard that line from a journalist before?'

He turned the conversation back to my moral duty to support this Palestinian football match and before he hung up I heard myself pledge to give his project some publicity. It was a pledge I was unable to keep; I broke my promise to a politician.

England set themselves a new World Cup record when they beat Iraq 8-0. The front page of the *Sun* said 'Iraq – you were Shi'ite'. In amongst the acres of fevered football coverage, there was not a single mention of Tony Blair's proposed 'Peace Match' between Israel and Palestine. However, most papers did carry different versions of a story about Tony Blair being on a 'junket' to Qatar to 'cadge' free England tickets. International journalists apparently 'boycotted' a Blair press conference at which he refused to answer the Iraq questions that would not go away. Internet news sites found that the combination of the words 'Blair' and 'Iraq' can lead to several strongly worded sentences in the comments section.

I wondered if he looked at all this coverage and gave any thought to what I had said. He had the opportunity to rewrite his legacy. I knew from our conversation that it wasn't going to happen. Until I could answer that key question – 'What big secret?' – that was exactly what it would remain.

That night, alone in my hotel room, while the highlights of England v Iraq played in the background, I re-read the leaked cabinet documents, trying to make sense of my disparate conspiracy theories. I wrote down my All-Time England XI and imagined if I was Tony Blair in 1997, how would I utilize those great talents to build a World Cup winning team for the future? On the television, England scored their first goal, a powerful header from England's young number 9, who ran to the corner flag pointing his finger into the air in the way that Alan Shearer always did. On the notepad in front of me, I wrote down a few ideas about what Robert Winston might be able to bring to the discussion. How might the nurturing of a baby develop world-class football skills from day one? Soon Iraq were two down; no argument about who was going to aim that free kick around the wall; England's tattooed number 7 was the only one who could bend it like Beckham. I had been leaked this particular player's contract, the results of his medical and fitness test, signed and dated by both parties. But only now did I notice the date: 'July 2002'. He had signed for Manchester United when he was only two years old! How can a scout spot a two-year-old's natural football ability? The ball can't have been more than four inches across; it probably had Thomas the Tank Engine on it.

On the television England scored their third; a neatly worked team goal that left the Iraqi defence split right down the middle. The cameras cut to the executive seats and there, sitting beside the Emir of Qatar, was Tony Blair, applauding politely at this English walkover.

'And probably mixed feelings for Tony Blair there,' said the commentator. 'Being reminded, perhaps, that sometimes, winning is the easy bit, it's the aftermath that is the real challenge.'

'Very much so, Barry. And that's as true in football as it is in the war on terror.'

'Ron, seeing Tony Blair there at this England–Iraq *rematch*, if you like, do you think enough evidence was brought before Parliament and the UN in 2003 for that declaration of war?'

'I've seen 'em given, Barry. I've seen 'em given.'

And I pressed pause on my remote control and stared at the former Prime Minister. Earlier that day I had been astonished to see that he had started following me on Twitter. And before long I would know what he was actually thinking.

In the zone

Assorted British Hacks v Arab Teenagers
Kick-about
Desert village of Qasa'hi – 8 December 2022

I had never quite given up hope of getting that call-up to the England team myself. OK, so I only played five-a-side with a bunch of mates on a Sunday night, but I still felt that a good national scouting system would surely have spotted my unerring striker's ability to put the ball away as it rebounded off the leisure centre wall after my first shot had gone well wide. I'd never seen any England striker do that.

I often attended the press conferences in advance of international matches and on each occasion a tiny part of me was crushed when the England manager didn't take me aside afterwards and ask if I'd consider playing for the national team. 'The thing is, Alfie, you might imagine that I have no idea who you are, but I saw you playing keepy-uppy with that beach ball in the car park last year and that's exactly the sort of skilful

ball play England needs in the centre of midfield.'
Another fantasy involved him rushing ashen-faced
into the press conference and saying, 'Oh no, my centre
forward has twisted his ankle and I forgot to arrange
any substitutes! Is there anyone in this press corps who
has his own England shirt with his name on the back,
which say, his son might have bought him for his last
birthday?' At which point all the other hacks turn as
one to look at me, and I stand and say, 'I won't let you
down . . .'

Although this had yet to happen, I joked that the
reason I still played every week was so that I would
be fully match-fit when the call finally came. But all
I ever hoped for as I drove to my game each week was
one moment during the hour; one split second when I
instinctively attempted a move or a turn or a shot, and
I pulled it off without quite knowing how I had done
it. A brief elevation into the zone; a split second of
pure *flow*; the 'ki' or 'chi' as it's known in martial arts,
which they describe as an ecstatic moment of physical
and mental rapture; when your body and mind operate
at lightning speed with total unconscious control and
you know you have achieved something you could
never do in a less focused mental state.

Obviously football managers have long understood
the value of Eastern philosophies and can often be
heard on the touchline furiously shouting at their

centre backs, 'Oi, Baz! Get your fucking yin balanced with your yang, you twat! If that dago tries to nutmeg you again, seek the higher spiritual plane of chi and find your pranayama, you fucking muppet!'

So the sight of any football pitch drew me like an addict; a kid's mini-goal in a back garden, a couple of sticks stuck in the sand at the beach, a painted line on a playground wall . . . 'Over here, kids, pass your ball and watch me lift it up with a little flick and volley it into the top corner . . .' But something isn't quite right and I'm leaning back too much and the ball goes sky high and over the fence into the neighbour's garden and the kids stand there looking at me in disgust because I've lost their ball. 'Oh, sorry. I'm sure they'll throw it back over eventually.'

I was really missing my regular five-a-side game while I was out in Qatar. I had mooted the notion of a kick-about with some of the other journalists covering the tournament, but they had only agreed to this as an abstract notion; any attempt to pin down a specific time or likely venue saw the numbers rapidly falling away.

In any case, our papers kept commissioning us to write articles; it was extremely annoying. I myself had been instructed to do a background piece about life in an ordinary Qatari village, far away from the gleaming new stadiums and the press junkets that had been laid on for the world's media. And so I headed out of the capital in a hired minibus with a driver and interpreter and a few other journalists and fixers who came along for the ride. We were deliberately venturing outside the officially approved zone, beyond the area covered by our FIFA-supplied maps, where they could not guarantee the ready availability of prawn sandwiches or bottled mineral water. To start with the road signs were in Arabic and English. Then they were only in Arabic. And then there were no signs at all. When we passed a semi-derelict building with a large painting of Osama bin Laden on the side, we could be fairly confident that we had travelled further than the authorities ever intended us to go.

The countryside was dry and dusty, with little out-crops of palm trees around an occasional oasis where a solitary building would have 'Coca-Cola' emblazoned on the side. Every so often we would pass a boy leading a camel or an old man with a couple of goats, and they would stop and stare at us in wonder as we zoomed past in a cloud of dust. The buildings were all one storey high, with no glass in the windows and the white paint cracking and peeling in the sun.

When we finally stumbled on a small farming community about two hours' drive out of Doha, there was a certain amount of incredulity that these aliens from another planet should have chosen to land here.

People hovered in doorways and stared at us as we climbed out of our tour bus. We should have bounded over to some village elder, introduced ourselves and asked if he would give us a tour, but when we did finally start to walk around, the locals seemed wary and suspicious of us. Wizened old men looked up from handlooms or where they sat weaving baskets, or mostly sat doing nothing at all, and we smiled and nodded as we walked past like Captain Cook touring a newly discovered island. Groups of bored teenagers followed us at a distance, wondering what we might be planning for their village. When our photographer tried to take their picture they turned away or covered their faces. We were definitely failing to form any sort of bond with the locals.

And then I saw it. Beyond a small mosque was a football pitch. A scuffed and misshapen dirt square, with large sticks for goals with string tied across the top. There were a few animals grazing around the edge, but it was still a football pitch. I dashed back to the bus and fetched a brand-new football that I had been keeping with me at all times. When the local boys saw this magical symbol their demeanour immediately changed.

'Do you want a game?' I asked, via our interpreter, and before he had even translated, they were nodding in eager agreement and other teenagers were appearing and heated discussions began regarding which of them would play in which position. And so in the heat of the Arabian peninsula, an improvised football match sprang up between eight fat British blokes, and eight Arabs aged between sixteen and twenty. Well, officially there were eight of them; it seemed to keep creeping up to ten, but we didn't mind. Nor were we particularly fussed about throw-ins or corners, since there were no markings and the ball continued to be played way out on the wing as far as a broken wall and some dry shrubs. Offside was also hard to organize; their first goal seemed to be allowed because their young striker had been played onside by a goat.

One boy had a smattering of English and declared loudly, 'Qatar one, England nil'. So my dream had come to pass! I was finally playing for England; I was representing my country, playing up front for the Three Lions.

Other villagers began to gather round – men and women, children and grandparents – until there were fifty or sixty people watching us and applauding worthy attempts on goal or good passages of play. Plus the amount of sweat dripping off the visitors was probably worth about three weeks' rainfall to the local ecosystem. But now they liked us, we had found a way we could communicate; we had a football, they had a pitch, and now the whole community had warmed to these strangers who spoke the international language of footy.

The locals played barefoot, we were all wearing trainers or canvas deck shoes, but still their ball skills were superior to ours. When any of them got the ball they would try to do something extravagant and over-elaborate, and the old white blokes would quickly regain possession and start to pass it around like a semi-organized team. It was a contest between a collection of gifted and energetic young individuals, and a disciplined team of plodders who kept their positions.

'Always remember . . .' said Jeremy from the *Telegraph*, 'the name on the back of the shirt is not as important as the name on the front of the shirt.'

'What, *BetPoker24/7.com*?' said Bill.

Jeremy's point was sound. The organized, passing team always wins, doesn't it? But stamina would also be an issue. Although we were not yet aware of it, this game was to experiment with the new two-hour time-frame, with no half-time and play continuing until a couple of the players looked close to death through dehydration.

And little did I know when I had fetched the ball from the minibus, that it would be in this game that I would experience the most perfect moment of 'flow' or 'chi' that I would ever know. A sequence of sublime touches, as if I was being controlled by some higher force, which culminated in the most instinctive, perfectly placed goal I have ever scored.

Forgive me for talking you through it step by step, but a moment like this only happens once in the lifetime of a mediocre football player like myself. It's not like I described it in detail to any complete strangers, like say, a Qatari taxi driver or the barman at my hotel in Doha.

The ball was passed to me in midfield with my back to goal, but I let it deflect off the inside of my shoe as I spun to follow its trajectory, using the impetus to beat another defender who was now in hot pursuit. With a couple of deft touches I beat another man and then with a burst of speed and a dropped shoulder I sent another lad the wrong way. I felt unstoppable, invincible, I had to keep going for goal and with the keeper coming out and a defender closing in on me, I skipped over a sliding tackle, looked up and chipped the keeper, who was expecting me to go for power. The whole world was in slow motion as that ball sailed upwards and curved into the back of the net. Although of course there was no net as such, and the goal went in off the string, but I still felt like Pelé and Maradona and Messi all rolled into one.

I turned and accepted the reserved handshakes of my fellow players. 'Great goal, Alfie!' 'Well played, mate!' 'Lovely individual goal . . .' and I pretended it wasn't such a big deal, but inside I knew it was a massive moment in my life; the best bit of instinctive football I had ever played and a sporting moment I was pretty sure would never be equalled.

'Qatar one, England one!' declared the local linguist, and I was reminded that I had scored for England; my name was in the record books, no one could ever take that away from me.

Our superior organization did indeed see us go several goals ahead. We were well drilled by Bill from the *Sun*, whose grammar was continually corrected by Jeremy from the *Daily Telegraph*.

'Whose marking who?'

'WHOM!'

'Get back! We've got less players than them!'

'FEWER!'

But as we tired they recovered from 5-2 down to 6-6 and were desperate to beat us. When two of our guys could not carry on any more, I told the disappointed opposition that we would have to stop with only 117 minutes on the clock.

'Penalty shoot-out!' declared the lad who had been keeping score. He then reiterated the idea in Arabic and all his teammates excitedly agreed and used their heels to create a penalty spot in the dirt, fighting over who was to take the first one.

I had been taking a much-needed rest in goal at the

moment the game ended, and so it fell to me to win or lose the match for England. But the goals were smaller than standard size, and by remaining on my feet I reckoned I stood a good chance of blocking a few shots with one part of my body or another. The whole village had gathered slightly too close to the goal and were cheering and chanting the name of their first penalty taker as he took the long walk up to the spot. 'Come on, England!' shouted a lone British voice behind me.

He took a short run-up, a little shimmy and a change of pace and he blasted it hard and low to my right. I had never been a goalkeeper and had no instinct for the position, but as I saw the ball coming I stretched out a leg and it caught the rim of the ball enough to send it wide. I'd saved my first penalty. The boy fell to his knees and I heard British cheers behind me.

Mark's haunting words came into my head: 'One Englishman always misses a penalty.' Sure enough our first attempt went flying over the string. I let in a second and watched a third go in off the post. Once again, England were losing a penalty shoot-out. After four penalties each, they only needed one more to clinch it. Then up stepped their smallest player. A frail-looking boy who looked low in confidence and had been harangued during the match by the older boys for a series of mistakes. On the touchline I spotted a woman I presumed to be his mother, praying and whispering to herself. If he scored this, Qatar would be victorious. He tried to block out the shouts and whistles as he focused on the ball on the spot. I decided that he was going to put it to my left, and resolved to dive like a proper goalkeeper and push it away. We made eye contact for the briefest of moments and then he ran up and kicked it with all his might. I had guessed right! The ball was flying to my left and I was already on my way down to block it. But something went wrong with the shape of my body and I landed with my ribs on the ball which momentarily stopped it before it popped out from the pressure and rolled over the goal line.

I could hear the cheers of the whole village as I looked around to see that I had let it in. The boy was a hero to his delirious team, who carried him shoulder high as the villagers clapped and cheered and jumped up and down.

And Jeremy came up to me with a smile, and said, 'That was big of you, mate!'

'What do you mean?'

'Cut the bull! I saw what you did – deliberately letting the youngest lad win it for them! Very sporting of you.'

'Yeah, well done, Alfie. Nice moment,' said another teammate.

'Oh well, you know,' I said. 'I wanted to make it look like I was trying to save it . . .'

'Yeah, you actually dived, even if you did look like a felled tree going over. But look at them all – it means the world to him . . .'

And I thought, 'I must remember to put them all straight about what actually happened.'

Their players came over and shook our hands and patted our backs and mimed the greatest moments of the match and we laughed and listened to the interpreter and explained that no, sorry, we couldn't come back tomorrow. But I picked up my leather ball and formally presented it to the match winner, and the young lad couldn't believe I was actually going to give him this football to keep. And each of them got an England jersey or a 'FIFA Press' T-shirt, which as generous gestures go was diminished by the fact that the disgusting tops were completely soaked through with sweat. But to our horror they all put them straight on, and proudly posed for photographs and the match winner was asking about the mystery name on his new England shirt as fellow villagers argued over which Premiership club featured 'Dad – 40'.

I had never expected that one of the best matches of the World Cup 2022 would be played on a dirt pitch in a tiny village two hours out of the capital, with no referee or linesmen, but still with more sportsmanship than the showcase tournament being beamed all over the world.

We formed a queue to rinse our heads under the water pump and somehow I found myself at the back. 'No, Bill, do not ask them where you can buy a pint of lager; this is a devout Muslim country.'

'I'm all for respecting other faiths and all that; but no lager after football? That's fucking ridiculous!'

Finally I felt the immense relief that was flushing my head underneath the cool spring water that must have caused this village to be built here in the first place. The spluttering pipe did its best to rinse the sweat from my hair, as I watched the water run away to a stone trough where the bubbles sparkled in the late-afternoon sun.

And then it struck me. A moment of pure clarity and inspiration – the thought simply came into my head from nowhere. I stood up straight and stared out at the shimmering horizon. 'They're all clones!' I said out loud. The only person who could hear me was the Qatari boy who had been cranking the pump and he gave me a puzzled smile.

'They're all clones,' I said to him. 'The England squad – it's so obvious! They aren't the secret sons or adopted apprentices of those great players; *it's actually them*; the FA, the Cabinet, Robert Winston, they went and recreated England's Greatest Ever Team!'

My teammates were nearly back at the minibus and, despite my aching bones, I ran after them.

'Guys! Guys! Wait, wait – I've just realized something!'

They turned and looked at me with some concern. They were standing in a row – there was Bill from the *Sun*, Mike from the *Express*, Greg from the *Daily Mail*, and John from BBC Online, and I was so excited at my epiphany that I wanted to tell them all there and then.

'What? What is it?'

Our driver started up the engine of the minibus.

'Er, that penalty I let in at the end? I'd actually been trying to save it for real.'

'Look away now'

England v Italy, World Cup Quarter-final

Qatar University Stadium, Doha – 10 December 2022

Gordon Brown became Prime Minister in June 2007. At first his premiership seemed to go well; he looked completely in control and totally focused on a well-thought-through agenda. He was riding high in the polls and poised to call the general election that would have given him a proper mandate and a full term. Then something seemed to throw him completely off course. What we know now, of course, a fact that only became known fifteen years later, is that he had discovered *the Big Secret*.

Brown went apoplectic. To suddenly learn that during his decade as Chancellor, his neighbour Tony Blair had secretly spent around a billion pounds recreating a team of English football superstars . . . well, eye-witnesses inside Downing Street say the swearing and shouting was terrifying to behold. Twenty-two human clones had been created, putting Britain at the forefront of biological innovation and research. But they were all English footballers.

'What about fucking Dalglish?' shouted Brown to his aides. 'What about Denis Law?' We could have made a team easily as good as the English one! Twenty-two players – we could have had eleven of each! But no, Tony fucking Blair makes them all English!'

Brown didn't sleep, he couldn't eat; he paced around inside Downing Street shouting the names of great Scottish football players to anyone who would listen.

'What about Jimmy Johnstone? And Archie Gemmill's goal against the Dutch? Tell me *one* England goal as good as that one?'

His advisors tried to get him back on track but he brooded and ranted for days. Eventually he resolved that now he was Prime Minister he would create an equivalent Scottish team. Despite advice that there was no longer the money nor the political will for another such project, Gordon Brown sat at his desk, drawing up lists of players and working out different permutations.

'Prime Minister? There are worrying signs of an impending financial collapse . . .'

'Hmmm . . . if we have Dave Mackay and Alan Hansen at the back, with Billy McNeill and John Grieg making up a flat back four . . .'

'Sir, we need to act urgently if we are going to forestall major bank closures and economic disaster.'

'OK, in central midfield I've got Souness and Strachan. But where do I put Billy Bremner?'

And now I myself had joined the elite club of those who knew the Big Secret. How many of us were there, I wondered. How did they manage to keep such information classified for so long? Had they all had to sign the Official Secrets Act? Was it considered a matter of National Security? Or was it simply that they were too aware of the avalanche of hostility that would come crashing down upon the first person to ruin England's chances of winning the World Cup?*

It was a surreal experience, watching this England team now that I knew who they really were. I felt a special privilege to be one of the tiny minority to understand what we were witnessing; to know what a miracle it was that this dream team had actually been brought together. Stanley Matthews passes to David Beckham; he floats a cross to Kevin Keegan, who nods it down to Bobby Charlton, who shoots to complete a fabulous hat-trick.

How was I supposed to write a normal match report

*Even Gordon Brown himself sat on the secret; his reaction to the discovery was only subsequently revealed by a disloyal aide. At which point Brown made his only comment on the scandal, emphatically denying her version of events. 'I never said that!' he thundered. 'I had Bob Wilson in goal, not Jim Leighton!'

of England's superb 7-0 victory over Norway in the first knock-out round? *Can you hear me, Edvard Munch? Vidkun Quisling!! Roald Amundsen? Thor Heyerdahl! Henrik Ibsen . . . your boys took a hell of a beating!* I was hamstrung by the enormous secret bursting to spill out of me. 'Don't you see?' I wanted to write. 'It was 7-0 because of who they really are. This is historic! This is as big as the splitting of the atom or a man on the moon! They have successfully cloned human beings!'

I had to admit I had something of a football fan's reaction to the revelation; because the prospect of England winning the World Cup again felt equally historic. I was thrilled at the realistic prospect that we might go on and win this tournament. Did I stop to think whether it was *wrong*? Did I think it was a cheat? Perhaps I was too blinded by my excitement at England's renewed chances, but I found myself reasoning that, despite all the paranoid secrecy and the extensive cover-up, the England set-up had not actually done anything immoral. They weren't fielding ineligible players, they weren't building the youngsters up on banned steroids. They had simply maximized the advantage the UK had gained at being the first country to clone a mammal, by cloning twenty-two more mammals who happened to be extremely good at football. Though I wasn't so sure of England's moral impunity that I felt revealing this secret would not be without serious ramifications. Rival countries might not view the revelation in quite such a benevolent light; it was quite possible that my secret could get England disqualified from the World Cup when they were finally in with a chance of winning it. In any case I had no actual proof; to go public I would need that one key document: a detailed confession, or incriminating minutes of some confidential meeting.

I had no idea whether Tony Blair personally managed his private Twitter account, and whether it had been his decision to follow me, but I sent him a Direct Message anyway. It simply said *You asked me 'WHAT BIG SECRET?' Answer: 'THEY ARE ALL CLONES.' Now will you let me publish the story in a way that you get the credit?* My guess was that he would never see it, that this DM would be deleted by the intern who had a full-time job blocking all the vitriolic messages from foul-mouthed trolls and George Galloway.

So in the meantime I felt constrained to write the same bald facts as every other football reporter: that England had already broken their record for the most goals scored at a World Cup, that they were the first ever team not to concede a World Cup goal in any of their first four games and had become joint-favourites to win the whole tournament. Now when England won their games, the television followed the numeral with the word in brackets to make it clear that it wasn't a mistake: Norway 0 – England 7 (seven).

I'd never been the sort of journalist to intercept mail, to hack phones or plant listening devices. Such steps could only be justified if one was investigating something of enormous public interest, such as international spy rings, corrupt governments or the England team's prospects in the World Cup finals. The FA had taken offices in a business complex down by the marina. I had got my press accreditation certified there, and had noticed the place was packed with filing cabinets and carelessly unattended computers. If only I could get an hour or so in there on my own to snoop around, to rifle through drawers and open computer files and finally pull out a dusty old-fashioned folder with 'Top Secret' stamped diagonally across it.

But of course the office was constantly teeming with FA staff. At night the whole complex was locked down, with security guards who looked like Vinnie Jones in a bad mood. Any approach would have to be during the day. But what were the chances that the entire staff of the Football Association were all going to leave the building at exactly the same time?

'Oh no . . .' I thought to myself. 'Don't make me miss an England game! Not now; not with this team!' On Saturday at 3 p.m. England would be playing Italy in the quarter-final of the World Cup. The offices of the

FA would surely be deserted as everyone decamped to University Stadium. And maybe, just maybe, there would be a solitary security officer at the door who was corrupt enough to let me in? I knew it was a long shot – a dishonest Qatari official out to make as much easy cash as he could during this World Cup – but there had to be an outside chance, didn't there?

I couldn't remember the last time I had missed an England game. Home or away, friendlies and qualifiers, I had watched them all in real time, either at the ground itself or on the telly. That impossible challenge of trying to get through the day without finding out the score and then watching the highlights; that never works. 'I know the score, but I won't tell you,' says a smug friend. Well they have gone and told you right there! Just from the lack of surprise in their voice; that's obviously a low-scoring home win; it's as clear as the intonation of James Alexander Gordon on *Sports Report*. Sometimes it's even more obvious. 'Oooh, I *won't* tell you the score, but you should *definitely* watch *Match of the Day* this evening.'

'No! Don't say it *like that*! That's clearly a surprising result, so while the score stays unsurprising, there is no suspense in whether it is going to change or not. You've ruined it now.' So just for future reference, if you are ever with someone who doesn't want to know the score of a football match, *do not even look at them*, do not move or breathe; it is too obvious a giveaway.

With a whole day to wait until my big chance to get inside the Football Association office, I had plenty of time to consider other means to try and fish for the proof I needed. I put in an interview request with the Chief Executive of the FA; I contacted the agents of some of the England players, but didn't hold out much hope. I wanted to share my secret with work colleagues, but since they were all professional journalists, I decided that wouldn't be the smartest way of protecting the exclusive of a lifetime. This secret was both wonderful and terrifying; it couldn't stay inside me, I had to do something about it.

And so when England kicked off their historic match against Italy, there was one empty chair in the press box. The quarter-final is traditionally when England are knocked out of the World Cup. By choosing not to be there, I couldn't help but think I was jinxing the England team; if they got eliminated now, it would all be my fault. But I had my own personal trophy to win; this was the one big story I had stumbled upon in my entire career as a journalist and it would never happen again. I had to make my name at this World Cup or watch my vocation fizzle out along with the print media that I'd confidently chosen as the perfect career path about five minutes before the Internet took off.

I approached the temporary offices of the English

Football Association at exactly three o'clock. England
v Italy would be kicking off this very second. I signed
into the building as 'Jules Rimet' and headed to the
lift. 'Heart, I'd like to introduce you to Mouth.' In my
pocket was a fat wad of five thousand Qatari riyals
with which to bribe the anticipated guard. 'Would
there be more than one?' I wondered as I turned into
the corridor. 'Would they be armed?'

It was worse than that. Sitting behind a desk wearing a mauve cardigan was the middle-aged English lady
who had been on reception last time. 'Yes, sir, how can
I help you?' she said.

'Oh, I thought everyone would be watching the
match?'

'The match?'

'Er, England versus Italy?? The quarter-final of the
World Cup? This *is* the Football Association, isn't it?
I haven't come to the offices of the National Trust by
mistake?'

'Oh, *the match*, yes, of course, that's right, I'm the
only one here. All on my own!'

'Well, I can come back another time if you want to
go and watch it?'

'No, it's all right. I don't like football.'

I contemplated waving a fat wad of Qatari currency
under her nose, but she had an RSPB calendar above
her desk, and they didn't feel like they went together.

I mumbled an apology that I'd forgotten the offices would be empty and disappeared back around the corner. Somehow I felt that James Bond would have handled it differently. He certainly wouldn't have found himself hiding in the tiny gap between two vending machines for half an hour. My reasoning was that she couldn't just sit there all day; she'd have to pop to the loo eventually. And when I saw her pass by, I'd grab my chance to slip past the vacant reception desk and into the empty offices beyond.

Thus it was that I experienced the entire first half of England v Italy squeezed into a six-inch gap, struggling to breathe in total silence. I learnt that Snickers was 'the official chocolate bar of the 2022 World Cup'. I watched the text scroll past the tiny screen of my phone, my legs turning numb as I tried to keep my size 11 shoes well out of vision. As a means of following a football match it was about as comfortable as Loftus Road. I remained sandwiched there in concentrated silence, staring at the updates from the BBC Football page, which described the events at the stadium in the driest, most detached language possible. I think the person writing them may have been my old geography teacher, so determined was the author to suck any interest out of the subject matter. This is how the BBC Text Commentary would have described the opening of *Raiders of the Lost Ark*:

3.00 – The credits end, indicating that the quest has begun.

3.01 – Indiana Jones enters jungle cave.

3.03 – Boulder rolls towards Jones. He takes evasive action.

3.03 – Jones retrieves hat.

3.04 – Jones exits the cave. Amazonian Indians await with weapons drawn. He takes evasive action.

3.05 – Jones returns to plane. A snake is in his seat. He takes evasive action.

Compare that with the excitement of listening to a football match on the radio. That is completely the opposite experience – the roller-coaster adrenalin-fuelled screaming of the commentator has you on the edge of your seat. The only problem is that you have absolutely no idea what is going on. 'HE-BEATS-ONE-HE-BEATS-TWO-HE'S-THROUGH-ON-GOAL-IT'S-ONE-ON-ONE-WITH-THE-KEEPER!' screeches Jonathan Pearce as if he's about to have a heart attack. OK, he may have forgotten to say which side 'He' plays for and which team is about to take the lead, but these details aside, it is an infinitely superior way of experiencing a live football match.

In my bag was a tiny pair of headphones that I could plug into my iPhone. I so wanted to hear rather than read, to get a sense whether England were playing well, to see if there was a reason why they hadn't scored yet.

But I had to be professional, I had to listen out for the receptionist coming down the corridor, to be ready at any minute to do the most illegal thing I had ever done as a journalist.

Perhaps she was never going to come. My anxiety was increased by England's apparent inability to find the net. Half an hour gone and still the score was 0-0. Italy are famously defensive; had England's success been dependent on their opponents taking risks and coming forward? It was impossible to tell from the sterile sentences scrolling up the screen of my phone.

Then right at the beginning of the second half, the text suddenly said 'Goal Flash!' At that exact moment I heard footsteps and saw her stride straight past and round the corner. Now I had to move immediately; I couldn't wait the five or ten seconds to see which team had scored, to discover whether England were one goal up or one goal down. I tried to read as I rushed down the corridor but somehow I had nudged the screen away from the website, and I couldn't stop to fiddle with it now.

Sure enough, her desk was empty and I was smart enough to work out the code to open the door. You had to press a large green button marked 'Door Open'.

She would not be able to see me from where she sat, but still I had to work fast. There was an inner office that looked important, and rather helpfully there was a photo of Greg Dyke with his family on the desk. The drawers to the desk were unlocked. I felt my hand shaking as I pulled the top one open. I knew this bit of espionage was unlikely to succeed; these were temporary offices, the FA had briefly decamped to another continent, they couldn't be expected to bring entire filing cabinets of incriminating documents all the way from London. But there might have been some prepared statement for what to do if the secret got out; a possible rebuttal strategy or damage limitation plan.

The top drawer contained a Hubba Bubba. The next drawer contained a wallchart of the Qatar 2022 World Cup, rather annoyingly taken from another newspaper. There was a big photo of the England team in the centre. At this moment that young team of miracles were either 1-0 up, or 1-0 down. Surely I could put one headphone in and discreetly listen to the second half while I tiptoed around these empty offices?

Disaster! I knew immediately from the commentator's voice that England were losing. The anxiety with which he described that Italian throw, the impatience with which he wanted England to regain possession. Fairly quickly he confirmed my suspicions that England had conceded. It made it so hard to concentrate on the job in hand, and I was edgy enough already from making my debut as a burglar and a spy. Being anxious that the

Italians were on course to knock England out did not help settle my nerves. 'Oh, get up you Italian ponce, stop wasting time!' I thought, 'Anyone can see you're not really injured.'

I glanced through the narrow pane in the door and saw the back of the receptionist who had returned and was busy on her computer. The computers, of course! They took an age to turn on; yet time seemed to be whizzing by in my ear. England could not unlock the Italian defence, and now the computer demanded a password. I tried various variations on 'Fo0tball', '3lions' and 'TheyThinkItsAllOver' but all to no avail.

It was then that I spotted a briefcase on the floor of Greg Dyke's office. It clicked open, and there was a file of official-looking documents inside. The commentator's voice seemed to increase in desperation as the end of the game drew near.

Here it was! *Strictly Confidential* said the final folder. On the radio England were repeatedly pouring forward, it kept sounding like they were about to score until the commentator's voice trailed off as an attack was stifled or possession was lost. *The contents of this file are of the utmost sensitivity and under no circumstances should be discussed or even alluded to outside the boardroom of the Football Association, even with the ordinary staff of the FA.* My hands were shaking as I read on: *Meeting of the English Football Association, held at the boardroom,*

Lancaster Gate, 7 April 2022 . . . The first few items were the usual mundane business of meeting management, but my eyes shot down to Item 6 and the upper-case warning two-thirds of the way down the page. Was this it? The smoking gun, the detailed self-justification – proof at last?

> Item 6. TOP SECRET. OBVIOUSLY NOT FOR OUTSIDE DISCUSSION. As previously discussed, England FA blazers are currently supplied by tailors in Leeds with the England emblem already sewn on. But considerable savings could be made by shipping comparable blazers from China, with only the stitching of the emblem done in the UK? Recommend proceed but observing strict media blackout.

That was it? Bloody FA blazers? There was nothing else controversial at all. And England were five minutes from going out of the World Cup at the traditional quarter-final stage, so my extraordinary story would be about an ordinary England team after all. Except here came England again in my right ear; even by the extreme emotions of this commentator, this was a new level of excitement – it was three against two, we had an extra man, yes, he played the right pass, yes, he can equalize now, but he passes unselfishly round

the sprawling keeper, it's a simple tap-in for England;
'GOOOOAALLLLLLL!'

I don't know who shouted the loudest; the commentator or me. My arms were still above my head and I was still jumping up and down when the receptionist hurried in to investigate the noise.

'What are you doing in here?' she said. 'How long have you been here?'

'Oh, sorry. There was no one on the desk when I came back a while ago, so I thought I'd come in and wait until everyone came back. England have scored!'

'You can't just wander in here, these are private offices!'

'Oh, I thought, since the reception desk was empty . . . But England have scored, so the match will go to extra time – they'll be ages now, I'll come back tomorrow . . .'

And I was gone. My covert expedition had failed, I had been caught where I shouldn't have been, but I didn't care. I felt a huge sense of relief that England were still in this tournament. The goal had been in the 88th minute, and I listened to the extra time as I walked to my hotel. And I jumped in the air as I walked past the marina, when England went ahead at 97 minutes, and then I almost kissed a woman in a burka when England got a penalty at 112 minutes, and I stood outside my hotel as it was taken and punched the air as England went 3-1 up with five minutes left to play. And then in the hotel reception I was surprised to be handed a large padded envelope that had been left there for me, and in the privacy of my room I tore it open as England played injury time but continued to attack. I spilled the contents out on to my bed and there before me was everything I could possibly want to know about the secret cloning programme commissioned by the New Labour government in 1998. Here were missing minutes of the relevant secret meetings; here were the initial laboratory reports, budgets, feasibility studies on doing to human beings what had been achieved with Dolly the Sheep. There were even confidential minutes recording which of England's greatest ever players were being considered for cloning. One day I would show this list to Mark, to watch his outrage that they overlooked Carlton Palmer.

And in my ear, England poured forward again, and in the last seconds of extra time, England scored a fourth goal; this fantastic team were going all the way, and here was all the evidence why, Tony Blair wanted the world to know it was down to him; I was jumping up and down at England's victory, at my victory: England 4 Italy 1, Alfie 4, Rest of the World 0.

And then I got a text from my editor saying: *Appreciate delay due 2 extra time, but can we have yr match report ASAP.*

Love versus Duty
(away win)

Spain v Brazil – World Cup Third Place Play-off

Al Wakrah Stadium, Al Wakrah – 17 December 2022

Dolly the Sheep had been born just ten months before Tony Blair entered Downing Street. At that point few people were ready to make the mental leap that cloned human beings were obviously coming soon. But the secret government minutes now in my possession revealed the new Prime Minister consulting with a select group of trusted politicians and advisors about how this new godlike ability might best be employed to the service of mankind.

'No, John, we are not cloning Princess Diana,' he told a disappointed Prescott.

'But Pauline would really love it . . .'

'I'm afraid that's not sufficient justification to break the UN convention on reproductive cloning. And I for one am not going to Buckingham Palace to tell the Queen that we are proceeding with this controversial procedure, just so we can bring her nightmare daughter-in-law back from the dead.'

'OK, what about Buddy Holly?' said Prescott. 'Or Lonnie Donegan? I used to love skiffle!'

The theoretical possibility of bringing back individuals from history greatly excited those in attendance.* But of all the amazing possibilities available to them, with the scientific and economic resources to recreate the geniuses of the Renaissance or the Enlightenment, the New Labour government of the late 1990s ended up spending the entire budget on one sub-set of historical figures. Not scientists to cure terrible diseases and save thousands of lives. Not great writers and philosophers to provide a deeper understanding of the human condition. No, they chose footballers.

Footballers. Twenty-two of the greatest players ever to pull on the England shirt; that's what they decided would do more good for the country than another Isaac Newton or Isambard Kingdom Brunel. A clone of Bobby Moore and a brand-new Stanley Matthews and a whole squad of footballing national heroes; all reaching

---

*The technology had advanced to the stage that even one tiny hair follicle from a long-dead personage was sufficient to clone that individual. Though if you were cloning Hitler, you'd probably want to take it from his moustache.

their peak at exactly the same time, thereby creating an unbeatable World Cup team and transforming the self-confidence and mood of the nation.

'It is incredible when you think about it,' said Greg Dyke, 'that we are in the uniquely privileged position of being able to recreate say, the philosophical genius that was Voltaire.'

'Voltaire?' said Prescott. 'Nah – we don't want him. Goal-hanger.'

'Straight up?'

'Definitely. And always offside.'

'All right. But shouldn't we at least discuss who else we could give back to the world. What about Gandhi?'

'Nah – he's a right dirty bastard.'

'Gandhi? Mr Man-of-Peace himself?'

'Oh yeah, sure he talked all that passive resistance shit, but get him on a football pitch and Mahatma was all two-footed tackles and elbows in the face. Footy can do that to some people . . .'

There were of course many logistical issues that would still have to be overcome. How would they disguise the players' identities? How would they recreate the environments in which those talents had learnt the beautiful game? As far as Tony Blair was concerned, these were all problems to be sorted out later. In the heady euphoria that followed Labour's landslide, the new Prime Minister believed anything was possible with the right resources and enough political will. Peace in Northern Ireland? Sorted. Create a team of World Cup winners? We're on to it. Prevent your Deputy from punching the voters? Well, two out of three's not bad.

Robert Winston was the first scientist Blair had turned to when he resolved to proceed with this audacious idea. After a brief chat about Dolly the Sheep and England's recent exit from the 1998 World Cup, Blair had asked him if it would be possible to clone eleven David Beckhams.

'Human cloning is certainly a realistic possibility, Prime Minister, but I'm not sure you would want to do that.'

'Why not?'

'Well, Beckham's a great midfielder, but you've got to have some shape in the team; defenders, strikers, a goalie; eleven Beckhams wouldn't work as a World Cup winning eleven.'

'No, I'm only saying that as an example. But would it be scientifically possible? How would you do it?'

'Well, I'd have Shearer up front, with Jimmy Greaves playing just off him . . .'

It was clear he was going to fit right in.

*

The audacity and enormous scale of this conspiracy fell into place for me over the course of one night, as I read through the reams and reams of secret files on 'Future Football' that I'd received from the mystery source working for the former Prime Minister of Great Britain. I trawled through the papers until dawn, my incredulity matched only by my professional shame at not having guessed earlier.

I learnt how the players' identities had been concealed at the single cell stage by painstakingly replacing specific genes relating to their facial appearance. Now Wayne Rooney's nose looked nothing like a potato. Gary Lineker's ears were tiny; you would not have recognized any of them from their faces – it was only the way that they played football that I had identified. Well, that and the comb-over.

The secret transcripts had revealed Alf Ramsey as the obvious choice as manager, although worries had been expressed about the problem of his clone's relative youth. Other possible candidates such as Walter Winterbottom and Bobby Robson had all been discussed, but the committee felt that Alf Ramsey had already proven himself in this department (even though this one hadn't). Brian Clough was considered but rejected as no one could quite bear the prospect of all those impressionists doing his accent all over again. Graham Taylor had apparently offered his services again, but the minutes were blacked out here, like the deleted expletives in the Watergate transcripts.

It goes without saying that well over half of the documents were made up of extended arguments about which players should make the All-Time XI. There were angry emails insisting it was madness to play Keegan alone up front, there were minutes of government meetings that had broken up in disarray at the suggestion that Nat Lofthouse could tuck in behind Ian Wright. I shook my head in dismay that so much of the Prime Minister's time should have been wasted arguing about this, and almost immediately got drawn into the debate, agreeing that Des Walker would be better at the back than Mark Wright.

I learnt how the players' nurture had been contrived to follow that of their prototypes as closely as possible: although of course that wasn't always practical or ideal. Returning Tom Finney to Preston North End would not have been the best way to pitch him against world-class opposition. But players from the North East grew up in the North East, often in the very same extended families. The cloning had all been done with the cooperation of the original players or their next of kin. Unsurprisingly some of them had initially been uncomfortable with the idea. But set against the ethical debates about 'playing God' and the weird notion of having another version of themselves walking around; set against the worries over legal identities and personal responsibility; measured against all of these very valid arguments was one incontrovertible factor. They all really, really wanted England to win the World Cup.

The miracle was not only that the scientists and politicians had turned this fantasy team into a reality, but that everyone involved had managed to keep it a secret for two whole decades. There had been one or two near misses; at one point Tony Blair was reported to have said he'd enjoyed watching Newcastle legend Jackie Milburn, which was not actually physically possible. What he couldn't say was 'No, not *that* Jackie Milburn. I meant the new one!' The original intention had been to field this team of miracles at the 2026 World Cup when they were at their absolute peak. But fears that the secret was close to being discovered turned out to be a factor in the last-minute decision to send them to Qatar and see how far they got while they were still comparative youngsters.

And now England's All-Time XI looked like they might go all the way and actually win the World Cup. Unless I broke the secret and ran my story.

This was the choice before me. Send my newspaper the exclusive that our national football team were in fact all genetically engineered clones and risk them being disqualified from the tournament at the moment of its climax. Or sit on the story, watch England win the ultimate prize, but for the rest of my life remain an under-achieving hack in a dying medium, wondering what might have been.

I felt numbed by the responsibility of it all. When I had started pulling at this loose thread, I'd had no idea that I was on to something so big. If the truth got England disqualified, then exposing it would only create misery and disappointment for millions of people. Does truth always have to trump happiness, or are some things best kept secret?

As England approached their semi-final against Brazil, I had stayed awake all night agonizing over which choice I should make. Normally I would have been worried about how our players would perform in this massive game, but for the first time in my life I was more worried about what I was going to do. Then early on in the match, we went a goal down, and part of me guiltily thought this might get me off the hook; if England were knocked out, I could reveal my great secret with impunity. But I hated myself for clutching at some private little consolation at the prospect of us losing, and when England scored two goals in succession, I instinctively cheered with joy like any normal fan. Gary Lineker beat the keeper with a rare header, at which point his all-time England goal tally drew level with Bobby

Charlton's.* But then, bang on cue, Charlton got England's second to seize his long-standing record back. Of course millions of ordinary fans had no idea that these legends were back scoring for England and setting new records, but everyone was so amazed by the result it would have been hard for them to be any more thrilled than they already were. The white shirts passed around the yellow shirts like it was Real Madrid versus Norwich City. With five minutes to go, England got a third; a perfect team goal deftly tucked away by the graceful midfielder only I knew was really Glenn Hoddle. England had beaten Brazil! They were in the World Cup final!

The news showed footage from Trafalgar Square where fans had watched the match on giant screens and then jumped into the fountains where they splashed about and sang all night. Even in Surrey, people recorded the highlights and then watched them after *Countryfile*. At the final whistle, Tom's texts were coming through one after the other. My replies must have seemed underwhelming and half-hearted; the texting equivalent of mumbling and avoiding eye contact. There were other messages from Mark and some of the

---

*At one point it was Wayne Rooney who held the record as England's greatest ever goal-scorer, but then his clone suddenly hit a barren patch. The scientists who'd tweaked his hair-loss gene had failed to include a code that caused the hair to suddenly reappear again.

guys from my five-a-side game, everyone expressing envy that I was out there witnessing it all. They had no idea of the dilemma that was staring me in the face.

In order to make me feel even more conflicted, one of the sports channels marked England's first appearance in a World Cup final for over half a century with a special feature on the history of our national side. There was John Barnes dribbling through the Brazil defence, David Platt's last-minute winner against Belgium, the sublime third goal against the Dutch in Euro 96, there was Bobby Moore lifting the Jules Rimet trophy; it was as if this programme had been especially compiled for me right now, as I decided whether these players should be given a second chance. I had to talk to someone about it. I resolved to wait until it was a civilized hour to call England, and then gave up and rang her anyway.

'This better be important,' said Suzanne, picking up the phone in the middle of the night.

And so, sitting in my pyjamas in my sterile hotel room, with the air-conditioning drying my throat out, I told her everything. How I had long held suspicions about this team, and how I had a file full of evidence that England's All-Time XI were now a living, breathing reality. My greatest fear, I explained, was that printing this story would get England disqualified from the World Cup final. 'Imagine what that might be like for Tom,' I said, which we both understood was my real reason for calling. 'If it was his dad that stopped England winning the World Cup?'

She thought for a moment and chose her words slowly.

'If you publish that story, your eleven-year-old son will be very disappointed in you.'

'That's what I thought . . .'

'But if you *don't* publish that story,' she continued, 'in fifteen years' time, your twenty-six-year-old son will be very disappointed in you.'

See, this is what always irritated me about her. I had rung up seeking a nice simple answer, but she had to be all thoughtful and wise. Even more annoyingly, she said the decision had to be mine, though she thought I should talk to Tom about the wider principle.

'OK, thanks. Sorry to have woken you up.'

'It's fine. I can see it was important . . .'

'All right, bye. Oh, er, and did you want to know who they've actually got in the All-Time England team?'

'No, it's OK, thanks.'

No wonder we never got married.

I sent Tom a message to Skype me when he woke up and then practised the gentlest way to break the notion that his father might be about to kill England's chances of playing in the final. I still had not found the right words when the electronic chirrup of Skype's ringtone made me jump.

He was brimming with excitement when he appeared on the screen; I think he had put on his England shirt especially for the call, bouncing around on his bed clutching a plastic World Cup ball. Behind him were pictures of his favourite players and I spotted one of my articles pinned up on his bedroom noticeboard. We hadn't spoken since England's defeat of Brazil and Tom was thrilled to report how people had spilled out of their houses after the result, running down their local high streets or waving flags out of the windows of speeding cars. 'The whole country has gone mad for it, Dad, you wouldn't believe it! A giant red cross has been painted on the White Cliffs of Dover, so the flag of England is the first thing visitors see.'*

'Great. Yeah. The thing is, Tom . . . I have this big story on the England team that I can't decide if I should publish or not . . .'

'Oh wow, do you know the line-up for the final?' he said excitedly, bouncing his souvenir plastic football off the wall and catching it again.

*The giant St George's flag did create some controversy, but those who objected to 'defacing a beautiful natural monument' were dismissed as unpatriotic killjoys. A few weeks after the precedent of painting the famous White Cliffs had been established, the symbol of England was replaced by a giant Nike tick.

'Well in one way I do. But it's not what you think. It's a scandal. A big scandal involving all of them. But if I let the secret out, England might be disqualified.'

He looked utterly confused and horrified all at the same time.

'What have they done?' he said slowly.

'They haven't done anything, the players are innocent in all of this. I'm sorry I can't tell you what it is yet, but now I have to decide which is more important. Everyone knowing the truth? Or England winning the World Cup?'

The Skype line was a bit erratic, and his face froze for a second in an expression of abject sadness.

'Will everyone know it was you that told on them?'

'Yes, if I make a claim, I can't do it anonymously.'

'But everyone will hate you. If you stop England playing in the World Cup final, everyone will hate you.'

'I know.'

'And everyone at school will know it was my dad who stopped England winning the World Cup.'

'I know.'

His eyes wandered from the camera. I think he may have been playing out this scenario in his head, imagining the pointing fingers in the playground, the licence this would give the school bullies.

'So why do you want to tell everyone?'

'Because lots of people have not been honest with

us. And if I have found out what they've been doing and I keep it a secret, that makes me dishonest as well.'

'But – can't you . . . ? The final is tomorrow. Do you have to do it now?'

My son wanted to postpone the hard decision. There was one thing he'd inherited from his father. He was staring down at his football, the Qatar 2022 logo was already looking a little scuffed and faded.

'Tom, you remember when you won that penalty, but you didn't think it was fair? Instead of scoring, you just kicked the ball out of play?'

Still he couldn't make eye contact. 'This is a slightly bigger game than that one, Dad.'

'But the principle's the same.'

'You're going to kick the ball out of play?'

'Maybe. Probably. Like you showed me . . .'

He was completely still now, all the early morning exuberance had been drained from him.

'Why does everything always have to be ruined?' he said, close to tears, and he slammed his computer lid shut and the call was over.

I felt haunted by the expression on Tom's face all day. I forced myself to finish my exclusive, still undecided as to whether it would ever see the light of day. I attached photographs of the original documents, I had quotes from the secret minutes; I even included Robert Winston's explanation to John Prescott about why they couldn't clone Roy of the Rovers. I read and re-read the material, alternately struck by the scale of this conspiracy and the massive dilemma before me, now that I had the power to expose it.

I went for a walk along the beach, I ate lunch alone, staring out at the sea, still utterly conflicted as to what I should do. I kept my laptop with me at all times, it seemed to get heavier and heavier as the day wore on. I watched the tide come in; the footprints where I had walked along the wet sand were washed away. I'd never get another chance like this to make my mark as a journalist, I would never have such an explosive exclusive in my hands again. But could I do this to them? Could I do it to myself? My personal dream had always been to see the England football team triumph in the greatest tournament in the world. That imminent and achievable football result would make me and so many people so deliriously happy that to crush that possibility seemed like a wantonly destructive and treacherous act. That had always been my weakness as a sports journalist; I cared too much.

So what better place for my sense of professional in-adequacy to be highlighted than at that evening's FIFA World Cup Press Awards? Sitting at a table in the huge dining hall, I joined in the half-hearted applause for a Dutch reporter and his sycophantic coverage of the 'excellent work' FIFA had done spreading football to undiscovered tribes of Amazonian Indians. I was too distracted to feel even the slightest sense of dis-appointment that I had not won anything for my worthy exposé on the football-stitching sweatshops of the Third World. Bill had entered his All-Time XI on football players with the rudest names (Seaman, Quim, Butt, Ball, Kuntz and Ars Bandeet).

The awards were being held at the Al Wakrah Stadium immediately before the penultimate game of the tournament. The World Cup Third Place Play-off is briefly a big deal for the country that finishes third. But even the other nation participating will immediately forget it; referring to themselves as semi-finalists from the moment they finish fourth. For the rest of us, it's an irrelevant annoyance; like stopping *Star Wars* before the climax and then watching a whole other film about Luke Skywalker's aunt and uncle if they'd lived. It would be a cynical journalist who suggested that the FIFA World Cup Press Awards had been invented to get us hacks to turn up to the most pointless match of the tournament.

'Fuck me, Alfie, that was an amazing exposé you wrote in the *Mirror*!' slurred Bill from the *Sun*. 'So you're claiming the Indian girl who stitches footballs gets *less* than the top players in the world?? I can't believe you didn't win. 'Cos till I read your article I'd have guessed it was the other way round! That Indian factory workers get two hundred grand a week, and Premiership footballers were on a dollar a day.'

'She doesn't work in a factory; her family are subcontracted to work at home. That's why the Factory Act doesn't apply. You clearly didn't finish it.'*

'You've never quite cut the mustard as a sports reporter, have you, Alfie?'

After a certain amount of alcohol, Bill's trademark witty rudeness dispensed with the 'witty' bit. 'You're a bit of a League Two hack really, aren't you?'

'Well, that's lovely of you to say so, thank you so much.' I smiled with an unoffended smugness that seemed to unnerve him.

Of course he had no idea what I was sitting on. A news story of such significance that his own newspaper would have nothing else on its first ten pages. None of the journalists at this event could have any idea of the secrets contained in my laptop that would blow every other story out of the water.

'So are you watching the game later?'

---

*To be fair, I hadn't actually done any of the original research on this wealth inequality scandal myself. The *Mirror* had subcontracted it to a journalist from an Indian news agency who ironically would have been on a fraction of the pay of his Western counterparts.

'Fuck that!' Bill said. 'I can't believe my article didn't win. Maybe they found out there was no such player as "Hans On-Der-Koch" . . .'

The only positive thing to say about that evening's football match is that England were not appearing in it. A demoralized Spain and Brazil, already exhausted and dispirited at having lost their semi-finals, lumbered around the pitch with no enthusiasm or self-belief. Inside the stadium the press seats remained empty while we chatted in the bar, casting occasional glances at the screens to see if anything interesting had happened. It never did.

No one was watching Brazil and Spain because they didn't matter any more. They were reduced to playing pointless football in a game so boring that most of the half-time analysis was spent discussing the Mexican wave. 'And interesting to note, Ron, that this Brazilian team has seven players who have a name beginning with "R" and ending in "O" – that's a new World Cup record!' All anyone cared about was the big game taking place tomorrow: England v Germany in the World Cup final. It would kick-off in less than twenty-four hours.

If, that was, it went ahead. Still I couldn't make a decision one way or the other. The file was all ready to email to the *Mirror*. The laptop was right in front of me, as I sat there looking far more worried than you'd normally expect for someone watching the third place play-off. The latest I could possibly send it would be this evening. I had told myself that I would make my decision at the end of the game. And then Spain v Brazil went to extra time.

I re-read my story yet again, trying to imagine its impact back home. I looked around at the other journalists in the room and wondered what they would do. It was hard to imagine any of them putting the progress of the England team above their own careers. Very few of them were even pretending to watch the football on the monitors any more, they were mostly drinking and complaining about the total sham of the FIFA Press Awards and the fact they hadn't won one.

I would definitely decide the moment this match was over, I told myself. A Spanish midfielder received the ball in the centre circle, then passed backwards to a defender to keep possession. No Brazilian players were pressing, but still the ball was passed back to the goalkeeper, who took several touches before tapping it out to the defender on the other side. If Mark had been there he would have put on his commentator's voice and said, 'And bizarrely, the pitch here seems to have two huge zeroes painted on it by the groundsman, and every player has the same number on the back of his shirt; again, zero, dash zero.'

'That's right Barry, this game has got nil-nil written all over it.'

It scared me to think that I had the power to significantly affect the happiness of the entire English nation. 'England Team Triumph in World Cup final' equals Elation. 'England Team Exposed as Genetically Created Freaks' equals Shock, Scandal, Disappointment. And remind me again what it is that people receiving bad news do to the messenger? Thank him? Congratulate him? Applaud his professionalism?

I didn't want to make millions of people back home unhappy. Being out here reminded me what I loved about my own country. I wasn't a patriot in the negative, 'disliking foreigners' way; I didn't think England was great and other countries were rubbish. But I felt lucky to come from an open and tolerant society, a place where corruption was not the norm and where a free press was fundamental to everything we believed in. These things make a country great more than the performance of the national football team. Keeping my story secret would actually be a very un-English thing to do, I reasoned.

On the TV monitors, extra time was over and so now came the most unexciting penalty shoot-out anyone could ever remember. Both sides scored all five penalties. It was almost as if neither goalkeeper could be bothered to try to save them. The shoot-out went to 'sudden death' although that phrase suggests an ending and it happening suddenly. The score was 5-5, then 10-10, then 15-15, then 20-20; the stadium started to empty before the winner had been decided.

But my eyes kept returning to my open laptop. All I had to do was press that button, and nothing would ever be the same again. (Although the way my fingers were shaking, I'd probably miss that key altogether and merely succeed in increasing the laptop volume.) I would be putting my duty as a journalist first and my love of the England football team second. I would be the star of my own life, instead of merely another extra in the crowd of this particular sports movie. 'Just once in your life, I'd like to see you make one difficult, definitive decision . . .' Suzanne had said to me when we'd split up. Dammit, why didn't she tell me which definitive decision I ought to make?

'Fucking hell, you're not still working, are you?' said Bill, coming over and plonking himself down opposite me. 'What's Alfie Baker's amazing exposé this week? Football shirts sold for more than they cost to make? Women's football not given equal billing shock? Bear Shits in Wood – World Exclusive!'

'You'll see,' I said. 'Who knows, you may even have to write about it yourself?'

'Ha! I doubt that very much.'

And I looked him in the eye as I calmly pressed 'send'

on my computer. I felt it important that the biggest decision of my life was made for the right reason. On the screens the cameras had cut back to the studio. Apparently the penalty shoot-out was over. I never did find out who won it.

Own goal

England v Germany – World Cup Final – (First Half)
Lusail Iconic Stadium, Lusail – 18 December 2022

This was supposed to be the day when I finally got to watch England in a World Cup final. Instead I was hiding in a pristine state-of-the-art toilet in Qatar's national stadium. On the plus side, it was a splendid toilet; no expense had been spared. There were fresh flowers, a soft white towel, a gentle fan maintaining the lightly perfumed air-conditioning at the ambient temperature. But sometimes not even the quality of a toilet cubicle is enough to lift the mood. Right now, it felt like the entire population of England despised me. And probably the rest of the world too, since they had all been looking forward to watching the biggest fixture of the planet's most popular sport. When my son had rejected my call, that had hurt most of all. It felt like some sort of death, confirming my status as National Hate Figure Number One; a pariah even my own child could not bear to talk to right now.

So this was probably not the best time to have a quick scroll down my Twitter timeline in the hope of finding some support for my courageous, honest reporting. *'U will die 4 this scum.'* *'Gr8, Thanx a lot traiter. U just gave Wolrd Cup 2 krauts* ☹☹☹' I am the reason England aren't going to play in the World Cup final. The nemesis of British football is personified by me. Of all the soccer villains down the ages; the violent players, the drunken managers, the corrupt FIFA delegates, no one will ever do their own side as much harm as that one English journalist; the man who grassed on his own national team and got England banned from the World Cup final. This will be the only day in my life for which I will be remembered; the headline of my short obituary; the answer to the only trivia question in which I'll ever feature.

The fact that all the other journalists in the Press Suite had affected disgust and outrage at my story only inflamed my feelings of injustice and persecution. They were furious with me because I was the parasite that had finally killed off our host. It was like the death of Diana; a generation of journalists hunted her all over the globe. But they feigned outrage towards the handful of paparazzi who closed down that particular sport for ever.

How bizarre it was that we all cared so much about the outcome of one particular football match, I thought. Thousands of migrant workers had been killed during the construction of Qatar's World Cup facilities. More people died building these stadiums than had played in them, yet that scandal was long forgotten in the media circus surrounding the tournament. London's Olympic facilities didn't take the life of one single construction worker and yet English patriotism is more closely tied to the performance of our football team than the hard-won rights and freedoms that save so many lives. It's insane, all of it. Football is the new opium of the masses; and I was both an addict and a dealer.

I heard someone enter the toilets. Did I imagine it or did the mystery visitor wash his hands in an angrier-than-usual manner? The hot-air dryer sounded more aggressive than normal, the door slammed particularly loudly as he left.

Was it possible, as many commentators were suggesting, that this was the scandal that would burst the bubble of football? That other, less-tainted sports would soon come to eclipse soccer, ending a century-long fashion for one particular game? It was a perfectly plausible scenario; there was no inherent reason why football should be the dominant global sport forever. Just don't let it be replaced by the long jump, I thought.

'Alfie? Alfie – are you in here?' came a voice I

recognized from the other side of the cubicle door. Bill sounded excited, friendly even, but I wondered if it might be some sort of trick. I would pretend to be a local; a Qatari employee, and so I cleverly improvised some Arabic sounding words to throw him off the scent.

'*Al qarnarqa dhobabi bin al salwa!*' I mumbled in a gruff deep voice.

'Oh, Alfie, thank god I've found you! How long you been in there – you didn't eat the shellfish curry, did you?'

I emerged to see Bill looking curiously pleased to see me. All the resentment and frostiness had evaporated.

'Alfie – the decision's been reversed! The final's going ahead! You're in the clear, mate!'

In a split second I had to take in the complex enormity of this news; its huge significance for football and for me personally, while being thrown off balance by the fact that Bill Butler was now being quite friendly to me. And in that split second I understood that I was suddenly a tabloid star in my own right; now I was someone he was proud to know.

An emergency FIFA board meeting had been held in the very stadium where we'd been waiting for the final. While I had been staring at the door of a toilet cubicle, a billion eyes had been on Michel Platini as the FIFA

President had emerged live on television to announce that the World Cup final between England and Germany was to go ahead only two hours later than originally scheduled. What was so refreshing was FIFA had made their decision solely on the basis of what was right and fair and in the long-term interests of the sport. These were honourable men; you could tell this from the iPhone recording of the secret meeting that one of them leaked on to the Internet about five minutes later. The rules of football were what mattered, not the FIFA billions at stake.

'Gentlemen, this emergency board meeting has been called to rule on an extraordinary situation that has only now been brought to our attention. It falls to us to make a judgement purely on the rules of the game, the honourable traditions of fair play and sportsmanship and the good name of FIFA.' There was a little coughing heard around the table at this point. 'We certainly will not allow our decision to be affected in any way by the huge amounts of money involved.'

'Absolutely.'

'Hear, hear.'

'Point of order, Mr Chairman,' interjected the Nigerian delegate. 'Can I just ask for clarification, a rough estimate of the huge amount of money that we are to put out of our minds altogether when making this decision?'

'Well, the money that will play no part in our ruling here today, would be . . . in terms of lost worldwide television rights, multinational sponsorship deals, global merchandizing and the sundry refunds and broken contractual obligations that may see FIFA being sued for loss of earnings . . . the amount of cash that we are *not to consider* here today, would be somewhere in the region of a hundred and forty-five billion dollars.'

On the recording you can hear an audible bang, as if someone's head hits the boardroom table.

'Of course, as directors of FIFA, we would never have gained personally from any of that money anyway . . . All those dollars would have gone directly back into grass-roots development of the sport.'

There was a lot of over-emphatic agreement.

'So completely disregarding the billions and billions and billions of dollars, and thinking only of the timeless principles of sportsmanship and fair play, do we think that today's World Cup final must be cancelled and one of the participants be disqualified?'

It was actually a much shorter meeting than many had anticipated. It was decided that the fairest thing to do would be to go right back to the original rules of Association Football as drawn up by the sport's founders in 1863 to see if there was any specific objection to the fielding of genetically identical human clones in competitive matches. It was very impressive how quickly the FIFA delegate managed to read right through the original rules to confirm that there had not. And it was on this basis that the 2022 final was allowed to go ahead after all.

So – it was game on! England v Germany in the World Cup final.

Can you believe it? I texted Mark. *A team of eleven human clones of the greatest ever England football stars, playing in the World Cup final in Qatar?*

No I still can't believe it. It's too ludicrous for words, Mark replied. *A World Cup final in fucking Qatar.*

A huge roar greeted the players as they emerged from the tunnel, England wearing red shirts, just as they had done in their finest hour. Soon I became aware of a commotion in the press box and an excitement in the stands as the England team went over to their fans behind the far goal. A huge cheer was building as a realization spread across the stadium. The names on their shirts had been changed! Gone were the pseudonyms under which the clones had had to live their lives to date; finally the England heroes could be proud of who they actually were. They lined up in front of the fans and then, pointing over their shoulders with both thumbs, turned as one, so the fans could see the back of their shirts. 'Banks', 'Charlton', 'Beckham', 'Lineker', read the inscriptions. This was it; the dream team of a million pub conversations, here were all the heroes for real, lined up to play for England in a World Cup final.

'This is incredible!' screamed the commentator seated in front of me, almost biting off his lip mic. 'Look at those names; every one a legend, every one an all-time great, every one a national hero!!'

It was an incredibly emotional moment. I felt this powerful nostalgia for things I'd never experienced first time round. I hadn't been born when Bobby Moore lifted the World Cup for England, but to see the late England captain out there, well it just brought it all back again. For in that moment, something special was shared between every English person who had grown up loving football. Something universal yet deeply personal, it was like an evocative echo of a time in our lives we all thought had gone for ever. Like a smell from early childhood, or a love song from your teens; thousands of us felt a deeply emotive connection with something lost; a heart-ripping grief for a youth that was gone for ever, here was a whiff of what used to be. To see these living icons of the past, with all the memories they brought with them, here together in their prime once more, it filled me with hope and sadness all mixed together and I was surprised to feel a strangled laugh slip out of my throat and then I realized I wasn't laughing, I was crying. And I glanced around to make sure that no one had heard me and I saw that all the other English journalists were crying too; rows of supposedly hardened, cynical tabloid hacks with tears streaming down their cheeks, all remembering when they were kids and watched long-ago World Cups with a now-departed dad or a wonderful mum who let them miss school for a midday England match because she knew how much it meant.

But how could any lover of the game not feel a lump in their throat to see Duncan Edwards, now exactly the same age as he was when he died after the Munich Air Crash, miraculously given another chance to realize his true potential in an England shirt? To see the reception this team was getting from the England fans behind the goal? Everyone was so happy for all of them.

'But oh dear . . .' said the commentator, 'Jimmy Greaves looks disappointed not to have made the final eleven.'

This was the England line-up for the twenty-second World Cup final. A huge cheer rolled around the ground as each player was listed in turn, their names slightly mispronounced by the Qatari announcer. In goal: England's number one – Gordon Banks. In defence: Bobby Moore, Billy Wright, Ashley Cole and Duncan Edwards. In midfield: Bobby Charlton, David Beckham, Stanley Matthews and Paul Gascoigne. And up front: Kevin Keegan and Gary Lineker.

The only thing that slightly diminished the epic

parade of our all-time greats was that, as well as asserting their right to play with their original names on their shirts, the players also opted for the style of kit in which they felt most comfortable. Kevin Keegan's skimpy tight shorts looked more like a pair of Speedo swimming trunks. Stanley Matthews' baggy shorts went down beyond his knees, and his boots seemed to come up to meet them halfway. David Beckham was covered in tattoos of important, meaningful words in Sanskrit and Hindi; some of them even spelt correctly. But it helped remind us that this was the team from down the ages, the ultimate in a century of English talent. Although of course five minutes after being moved to tears by the miraculous return of these all-time heroes, my work colleagues had already begun arguing about the FA's final selection.

'I can't believe they went for Keegan over Shearer! And how can you know which Gascoigne is gonna turn up? It's gotta be Bryan Robson there for me every day of the week . . .'

'Nah – when Gazza's on fire he can turn a game; you can always swap him for Tom Finney at half-time . . .'

The discovery that human cloning had been a reality for more than twenty years was also a massive international news story in its own right of course. The ethical and spiritual implications for mankind were supposed to be scrutinized on a special edition of the

Moral Maze on Radio 4 with Alain de Botton and Richard Dawkins, but they just ended up arguing about whether Colin Bell could play up front with Teddy Sheringham. Any dissenting voices about British scientists playing God, or mankind crossing into a dangerous new era of genetically modified humans were drowned out in the excitement about this football team, their progress to the final and the prospect of England actually winning the World Cup. It had taken billions of pounds and twenty-two scientific miracles, but finally we seemed to have the best player in the world for every single position on the pitch. England were unbeatable.

Perhaps that same over-confidence got to the players.

Because straight from the kick-off, I was shocked to see England struggling to get into the game. Germany played skilful flowing football; they kept the ball well, moved and passed quickly to feet. In the third minute they forced a corner, easily headed away by Duncan Edwards, but it was still a warning. I found that I had to stop myself welling up every time Duncan Edwards touched the ball. He had made it into this team because he was a great footballer, not because of the tragedy of his early death or the mythic quality of the Munich Air Disaster.

'Oh look, he's kicked it again! Duncan Edwards lives – and he's playing in a World Cup final . . .' and I collapsed into whimpering sobs at the poetry of it all.

After seven minutes I became aware that England had yet to get out of their own half. We were good but our opponents were better. A quick passing movement saw the German number 10 pick up the ball at the top of the D and for a split second I thought he was going to turn his marker and get a clean shot on goal. But then a brilliant tackle from Bobby Moore took the ball from right under his feet, and I found myself both applauding and laughing as the German blatantly dived in search of a free kick.

My laughter was cut short by the referee's whistle. The free kick had been granted! On the monitors in front of me, the replays showed the referee had got it completely wrong and a couple of England players were still complaining when Germany quickly took the free kick and scored. Half the stadium erupted. Germany were 1-0 up, their players were celebrating and England had been cheated.

The greatest England team of all time had been on the pitch for seven minutes and they were already losing to Germany. West Germany's equalizer in 1966 was from almost exactly the same spot. Their only goal in the 1990 semi-final was from a free kick right outside the box, we should have been ready for it.

'That's just what this game needed!' said an American commentator seated behind me. 'An early goal from the underdogs.'

'Underdogs?! By what token are the Germans the underdogs? World Cup winners four times, World or European finalists fifteen times! – this is England's first final away from home!' I was only supposed to think this; I wasn't supposed to stand up and shout it at the American while he was trying to do his live commentary.

But it made me realize that the neutrals around the world were cheering for Germany. Even though FIFA had declared our team legal under the rules, the exposure of this secret, gene-meddling master plan had made the rest of the world cast the English FA as some sort of evil scientists. A German win would be seen as a victory for honest hard graft, natural talent and superior tactics. If England won, they'd say it was because of what had been done in the science lab, not on the football pitch.

A stunned England kicked off and at last made a couple of forays around the edge of the German penalty area. Paul Gascoigne made a wonderful mazy run but ultimately attempted to beat one defender too many. Bobby Charlton tackled their big centre back and laid the ball off to Lineker, whose shot was blocked. For ten minutes England looked slightly more confident and I felt able to enjoy the miracle of seeing Billy Wright crossing to Ashley Cole who passed to Stanley Matthews who laid it off to Keegan who passed back to Beckham. Now we would see what these players were made of; greatness is revealed not in unmitigated success but in response to adversity. An England walkover would not have made for a great final. We conceded first in '66, and 1990, and got back into the game on both occasions.

Except that this German team was clearly very, very good. There was a reason they'd got through the 2022 World Cup with almost as many goals as England; it was not good luck that had seen them thrash great footballing nations on the way to the ultimate match.

In my pocket I felt my mobile phone vibrate, and saw a predictably negative text from Mark pop up: *I knew this would happen*. That was so typical of him. I sent him back a slightly longer text than he might have expected.

What, you knew that your best friend would expose England as a team of clones just as they faced their greatest rivals in the World Cup final in Qatar? And then England would go 1-0 down?

No – mainly the last bit. Even our greatest 11 players can't beat the Germans.

This last sentence particularly stung. Our finest ever players seemed to be lacking something when it came to the ultimate test. It couldn't be luck that Germany's record was so much better than ours. They had won 80 per cent of their penalty shoot-outs while England had only won 15 per cent. Is there something self-doubting about the English character that has seen us always under-achieve? Is there something in our DNA or upbringing that keeps making us blink at the last minute? Perhaps the pundits would cite the differing philosophical traditions of our two cultures: England's John Stuart Mill, very much the individualist, not a team player, whereas the Germans with their Hegelian dialectic, trained to emphasize the absolute idealism of the all-inclusive unit. 'Well this is it, Barry.'

I thought back over other historic England v Germany encounters. Lineker's equalizer in 1990. Lampard's disallowed goal in South Africa 2010. Bobby Moore's worst ever performance – as Terry Brady in *Escape to Victory* starring Sylvester Stallone, Michael Caine and Pelé. That match was written by Hollywood screen-writers and still the best England could manage against the Germans was a draw.

Now a slightly under-weighted pass from Keegan was cleverly anticipated and possession was lost unnecessarily on the edge of the centre circle. A quick pass to Germany's stocky little number 10 and he was off. He shimmied past two England shirts with ease, then beat a third as he set off down the right wing. This amazing run would indeed take him all the way to the England six-yard box, but the American broadcaster behind me was not to know that and his commentary peaked too early. Already screaming at the top of his voice, his larynx had nowhere else to go as the German number 10 continued to weave and dazzle his way towards the England goal. I sat transfixed; like Barnes in 1984 or Maradona against England in '86, it was clear it could only end with a goal. As the Germans celebrated, the high-pitched screams of the commentator actually became inaudible to the human ear, nearby dogs would have begun howling along.

It was possibly the best goal ever scored against England, but that didn't make it any easier to take. In fact I was already irritated by the England fans that I predicted would one day vote for it as the greatest goal of all time, as if making a point about their magnanimous ability to appreciate true genius despite the tragic context of their own team's defeat in a World Cup final.

Because that is what was staring us in the face. It may have meant nothing to the other journalists, applauding the replay of the goal, but Germany were now 2-0 up in the World Cup final and I was entertaining the unthinkable prospect that we might well lose this match. 'And Britain will just be grateful to get to the end of first period!' said the American commentator behind me, finally having got his voice back.

This bloke had been starting to get on my nerves when we were 1-0 down, but now it was intolerable.

'England's offence is not finding any real estate in the German last quarter.' What?! None of that sentence makes any sense. 'There's a real chicken-wing battle going on by the midfield stripe.' Again, that is not any language I recognize. 'That's what they need field-side: a possession receiver who can show some wheels.'

Obviously if England had been winning, I would have entertained this cultural quirk with amused good humour. But England were losing 2-0 and a bit of trans-Atlantic terminology momentarily became the focus of all my ill will and disappointment.

'It's called half-time!' I shouted at him. Like a true professional, he kept talking into his microphone, but gave me a quizzical look as if to suggest that my behaviour was somehow not acceptable.

'It's called half-time. Not "end of first period". And what the hell is a "possession-receiver"?'

I think at some level I was cross with this American for still being neutral. According to historical precedent, when we were losing to the Germans, the Yanks were supposed to join our side and help us turn it round.

As England tried to find a way back, I started to doubt the entire strategy of recreating the best players in every position. I've heard it argued that you don't want too many geniuses in one squad; that the most effective teams have been built around one or two superstars. Perhaps there were divisions in the dressing room? Maybe some of them resented the way that others in the team had previously earned £30,000 a week, while they had been lucky to get a ten shilling win bonus and their bus fare home.

'If we could just get to the end of first period,' I thought. 'Half-time, I mean, damn! If we can just get to *half-time*, then we could change tactics, make a couple of key substitutions, and maybe we'll get a bit of luck with a couple of penalties and two German players sent off.'

Now Germany were slowing the tempo of the game right down, the energy was being sucked out of the England supporters. On the close-ups on the monitors, they looked hot and uncomfortable, wrapped in flags or cumbersome fancy dress. (I was never entirely sure about the good taste of England fans dressing up as crusaders in an Arab country.) The perennial brass band kept playing the theme to *The Great Escape*, but it sounded tired and the chorus of 'Eng-land!' was half-hearted and forlorn. In any case that film doesn't end with a great escape, it ends with the English being massacred by the Germans.

Finally a wildly optimistic long-range shot came off a defender's leg for an England corner. Here at last was a chance. Beckham raised both hands in the air as a secret signal. But what if the Germans had broken our code? Maybe their crack mathematicians and linguists had spent hours and hours studying our arm signals and had worked out that Beckham's two-handed signal meant 'I am going to kick the ball into the penalty area. Try and get a goal.'

Beckham kicked the ball into the penalty area, as they were probably expecting. I saw that Keegan had lost his marker! He leapt up to meet the perfect cross and powered a header that had the keeper beaten. The ball bounced off the underside of the bar and landed behind the line as the England players celebrated. Goal! We're back in it! I was out of my seat cheering as the ball was belatedly hoofed up field by the German goalkeeper. But then that instant puncturing of elation when you realize a goal might not be given. Surely it had crossed the line? The England players were urging the referee to talk to the linesman but the assistant was already shaking his head and mouthing 'no' in that really annoying over-emphatic way. I felt my hands grip my face. He was so wrong, it had definitely been a goal; it was an outrage, a disgrace! We watched the replay on the monitor. Oh, the ball had *not* crossed the line. It was completely the right decision. 'Why did they have to introduce goal-line technology?' I thought. 'It's completely ruining the game . . .'*

---

*It was later calculated that in the tiny margins that can affect the angle of a shot, the deciding factor that prevented this header from crossing the line was Kevin Keegan's perm.

With some England players still attempting to argue with the ref about the unarguable video evidence, the German midfield were breaking away and England looked stretched out of shape again. Ashley Cole chased the stocky German number 8, but was stuck the wrong side of him. Banks was forced to come out to narrow the angle but the striker passed across the box to the unmarked white shirt running in from the left. Like a dog running out into a busy road, you could see what was going to happen, but you felt powerless to do anything but watch. The ball was perfectly struck and the net came alive, detonating the crowd behind.

It was over. Three nil down before half-time; there could be no coming back from this. All that effort, all those millions of pounds, the research, the secrecy, the political machinations, the scientific know-how that had gone into this incredible project and still our best ever was not as good as this year's Germans. In fact the outcome was going to be the worst of both worlds; the foreign press would portray England as cheats who were nonetheless beaten by a more talented, traditional team.

And then it felt as if I was the only person in the stadium, and all I could think was that my greatest wish was never going to come true. England were never going to win the World Cup in my lifetime. Because if they couldn't win it with this team, when would they ever? Never, that was the answer, England were never going to win the World Cup again. In that moment it felt like all those years spent following the team had been a pointless waste of time. The story is supposed to go; 'they lose, they lose, they lose but finally they win'. But no, they just lose again. What an idiot I had been to imagine there was any sort of justice or narrative logic to any of it.

Despite the searing heat I felt myself shiver, and realized that my phone had vibrated in my pocket. Who on earth would be contacting me at a moment like this? A comforting text from Tom maybe? A furious missed call from Greg Dyke? Or a warning from the police that death threats were now being made against me on social media? It was a direct message on Twitter. It must be a fake, I thought; a hoax account. Why would I get a personal message from the President of FIFA? *Mr Baker, congratulations on your exclusive. Why don't you join me in my private suite for a half-time drink?* Someone is winding me up, I thought, like that time Mark did a double bluff by shouting 'Goal!' loudly when I'd popped to the toilet and in fact it had been a goal. Surely the President of FIFA doesn't follow me, just one of thousands of football writers around the world. And even if he did, why would he want to talk to me in the middle of the World Cup final? The clue was in the message. Because of my exclusive. Because it genuinely *was* from the account of Michel Platini; he had millions of followers and the hallowed blue tick of Twitter authentication and a link to the official FIFA website. A couple of click-throughs soon revealed that he'd been following me since *before* my story had even broken. I was still wondering how to respond when another direct message came through that presumed that there was no choice for me in this matter. *A member of our staff will collect you when the whistle blows for half-time.*

The last few minutes of the first half were hard to watch in every sense. England were looking nervous and shell-shocked, while I couldn't concentrate for glancing over my shoulder for some approaching FIFA apparatchik. I imagined a pair of burly men in dark suits with sunglasses and earpieces, pacing menacingly down the steps towards me. In fact the person who was to lead me away did not approach as I expected, but had been sitting close by throughout the first half. And on the stroke of half-time she stood and introduced herself and I duly followed her like a nervous schoolboy. She was dressed like those Emirates air hostesses who stand in line as the Arsenal team come out of the tunnel, just in case one of the Gunners wants to order some duty-free on their way on to the pitch.

A final glance back saw the German team enthusiastically jogging off to the tunnel, while England heads hung low and shoulders drooped.

I followed the FIFA ambassador through a series of windowless corridors. Security guards stiffened as we dared approach, but were instantly transformed into fawning doormen as my escort waved her special pass.

'Are there a lot of journalists going?' I asked as I scurried behind her.

'No, just you,' she said without looking round.

'Blimey, so what is it, like a reception for lots of different interest groups?'

'No, just you,' she repeated, and a set of double doors nearly hit me in the face.

Eventually we were at the threshold of the inner-most cave. My guardian would come no further, but offered me a small plastic tray in which I was to leave my mobile phone and 'any other cameras or recording devices'. Under the watchful eye of the knights who stood guard at the inner sanctum, I duly did so. Then she knocked the door and sent me in alone.

And there was Michel Platini, standing and looking slightly fatter and scruffier as celebrities always seem to in real life. He was less impressive than I had expected for such a powerful man; the player who had been master of the French midfield looked somehow less comfortable in a suit and a swanky office.

This most exclusive of executive boxes might as well

have been in a plush suite back in Switzerland with the football projected live on to a giant screen where the tinted window stared silently down on to the distant pitch. So sealed off and immunized was it from the atmosphere of the ground, it felt like we were utterly removed from it all.

'Ah, Monsieur Baker!' he said. 'We wanted to meet the man who broke the football story of the century!'

I was irritated by his use of the royal 'we', but put it down to English not being his first language.

'The President was keen to meet you . . .' he continued. Although the words sounded pompous, the man himself seemed nervous and embarrassed about something.

'Well. Er, now you have . . . ?'

He avoided eye contact and at that moment I realized we were not alone. On the far side of a large wooden desk, a large leather chair swung round and I jumped as I saw a frail, bald old man sitting there. It took me a second to recognize him. There was the ghost of football past, clearly still at the centre of football present; the Emperor of Planet Soccer, the Wizard of Oz, the man I had once blamed for all of football's ills. Sepp Blatter was here.

'Michel. Get Mr Baker a drink!' he said, without even looking at the man I thought was supposed to be FIFA President. 'And I will have my usual.'

'Of course,' said Platini, and he scurried across the room and poured two whiskies from a crystal decanter.

I was dumbstruck; struggling to process this, to comprehend why Blatter was here and why the former President of FIFA should have authority over the man I thought currently held that position.

'More ice, Michel! More ice!'

'Of course!'

Blatter's face was thinner than I remembered it, the skin drawn more tightly around his skull. Finally I attempted to form a sentence. 'But you resigned? FIFA moved on?'

'That's right. I resigned!' and he gave out a little chuckle. 'But *you* of all people must understand that everything is not always as it seems . . .'

I felt a little light-headed and wondered if the air-conditioning was also pumping oxygen into this room.

'It was necessary for appearances' sake. But everyone at FIFA understood that I had far too much information . . . knowledge about the game, I mean. So it's only on the outside that I am not regarded as President for Life. A former football legend makes for better PR than this frail old man, *n'est-ce pas*, Michel?'

Platini managed a forced smile.

'But now you are telling me,' I gabbled. 'You know I am a journalist!'

'That's not the story you are going to publish next. Sit down, Mr Baker. We have plenty of time. Unfortunately, like the kick-off, the beginning of the second half is going to be delayed . . .'

I really felt he should have been stroking a white cat and looking at a scale model of a volcano that opened up to reveal a nuclear missile launcher.

'The second half is going to be delayed, Mr Baker, because of the next news exclusive you are going to reveal to the world's media. Congratulations on your first triumph, by the way. We felt that eventually someone must surely see it.'

'You knew?'

'Of course we knew! There is nothing that happens at the English FA that we don't know about . . . My god, their meetings are so boring!'

After everything I'd learnt about FIFA, I don't know why I was still shocked to learn that they had been bugging the Football Association. 'Who do you think was leaking you all that information?' he continued. 'Those little clues to keep you on the scent?'

'That was you?'

'The English FA were constant critics of FIFA. Every time there was another allegation from Greg Dyke, we sent a little warning shot to remind them that they had a few dirty secrets of their own . . .'

'But somebody had me arrested!' I protested. 'They hacked my computer—'

'I know!' laughed Blatter. 'English harassment is so quaint! In most other countries you'd have been shot through the head and dumped in the river.'

There was a big cheer from the Germans in the crowd; in the stadium I could see the goals from the first half being replayed on the giant screens.

'But you see, Mr Baker, you only got half the story. Yes, the England team are all clones of your country's greatest ever players—'

'What? Are they on steroids too? Did they make two clones of each of them to swap them round at half-time? Is there another scandal about them I missed?'

'Why do you English always put yourselves down like this? Not England – your opponents! You wrote that there were eleven miracles on the pitch. Look at the screens, Mr Baker. Can you not see it? Can you not recognize eleven more miracles in the colours of Germany?'

My brain misinterpreted this statement several times over in the microsecond that it took to process it. *Eleven more miracles in the colours of Germany* – does he mean the England reserves have come out in the wrong shirts? Does he mean that it's miraculous in a metaphorical way that Germany are so good? NO, NO,

NO – he means that the German players are all genetically reproduced clones too!! I stared at the tiny figures casually passing the ball about in the centre circle, my mind tripping over itself as it struggled to make sense of it all.

'Like us, the Bundesliga had moles inside the Football Association and knew about the FA's audacious plan back in the 1990s. They couldn't allow England to be the only team picking the very best players. So a newly unified Germany embarked on a genetic duplication programme of its own . . .'

Now it all made sense. No wonder Germany were winning 3-0, no wonder they were on the way to yet another World Cup victory.

'So the Bundesliga cloned the greatest ever German players?' I was shaking my head with astonished disbelief as I said it. 'Typical England. We have the idea and then someone else goes and does it better than us. So who have they got? Beckenbauer? Müller? Klinsmann?' I squinted through the window to see who I might recognize.

'Ha! Bless you for such limited imagination. You still don't get it, do you?' he laughed to himself. 'Germany saw the idea through to its full potential. Sure, everyone in that team was born and raised in Germany. Because it was Germany that had the vision to clone Pelé and Maradona and Eusébio and Cruyff and Zidane to put all of the world's greatest ever players into the German national football team!'

This was the moment I really should have dropped my whisky glass and heard it shatter into a thousand pieces on the floor. Blatter seemed to be taking some sort of perverse pride in the logical perfection of this plot, as if by simply imparting the information he could somehow take some of the credit for it. 'Michel Platini didn't quite make the grade, did he, Michel?'

Platini looked away and kicked a chair leg in disgust.

'You wonder why David Beckham had such a running battle with Germany's number 7 in the first half?' continued Blatter. 'Because the German number 7 is also David Beckham. He was trying to mark himself!'

England were in the World Cup final against the eleven greatest football players ever to have lived. Any sense of wonderment at this footballing impossibility was suffocated under a combination of shock and outrage.

'But – but that's cheating!' I stammered. 'Pelé is Brazilian. Everyone knows that. Zidane is French.'

'Actually Zidane's parents were Algerian, but he played for the country he grew up in. Just like all those German players out there.'

The old man's logic did nothing to assuage my burning sense of injustice; the outrage I felt that England were 3-0 down against a team that everyone thought were ordinary Germans.

'But it's not fair. We could have had bloody Giggs on the left of midfield!' Sure, what England did was audacious and unprecedented. But at least we did it with Englishmen. 'If Germany have people from all over the world – well that's just cheating.'

'Is it? What does it mean to be German or English? Are you demanding some sort of German racial quali- fication? I thought England fought and won a war against the Germany that thought along those lines?'

On the giant screens I recognized the distinctive passing style of the German David Beckham as he floated perfect cross-field balls to his fellow country- man Johan Cruyff. Blatter began to lecture me on how England's own national character was to blame for our situation at half-time.

'England is historically a nation of immigrants, and yet you never embrace this. It has been one of your strengths that you welcomed everyone from the Huguenots to Bangladeshis. But when you used your brilliant British scientific know-how to create your greatest possible team, what did you do? You turned back into Little Englanders . . .'

Now I momentarily worried about the Bond-villain quality to my host; don't these characters normally ex- plain the fiendish plot in every detail right before they have you put to death? England coming this far and then losing, that felt pretty much like the same thing.

'I still don't understand why you want to tell me all of this . . .'

'Well, the problem is that it's making for a very one-sided World Cup final. If the truth was to come out before the start of the second half, it would switch the support of the crowd, and make the England team feel like they were the underdogs instead of the favourites.'

He gestured to Platini who pushed a file across the desk towards me.

'There is all the proof you need. The moment this story breaks on your newspaper's website, we will delay the second half for our investigation. Then the whole world will know about it before FIFA allows the match to continue forty minutes later. My own involvement in all of this will remain secret until my promise of the World Cup in Qatar is finally over.'

I picked up the file and opened it like some precious ancient manuscript. The story had already been written out for me to save time, albeit with slightly cheesier tabloid puns and subheadings than I would have chosen myself. 'Double Deutsche! Germans in Cloning Soccer Shocker'; my 'half-time world exclusive' was preloaded on to a memory stick for me, all ready to be posted online with supporting evidence and photos.

He indicated an empty desk with a computer and a phone.

'But be quick. FIFA's second board meeting of the day will commence in ten minutes. We will give the second half the official go-ahead at 7.15 p.m.'

I think I returned a numb half-nod.

'It should make for a very interesting second half . . .' he said.

By far the greatest team the world has ever seen . . .

England v Germany – World Cup Final – (Second Half)
Lusail Iconic Stadium, Lusail – 18 December 2022

'TWO DAVID BECKHAMS! THERE'S ONLY TWO DAVID BECKHAMS!' The chant had struck up at the England end, but now the Germans were singing it too. And while twenty of the world's greatest players continued warming up for the second half, one midfielder from each team broke away and began walking slowly towards each other.

'TWO DAVID BECKHAMS! THERE'S ONLY TWO DAVID BECKHAMS!'

The whole stadium was singing it by the time they came together. They paused to regard one another for a second, and then English Beckham stepped forward and offered his hand to German Beckham. An explosive cheer went up as the two embraced, red shirt and white shirt, two people; one talent. Now the English and German teams stopped warming up and simply stood there applauding. The two Beckhams waved at both sets of supporters, and then they turned towards the VIP section of the stadium, where the cameras picked out the original, forty-seven-year-old David Beckham, sitting beside his grown-up kids.

'*Three* David Beckhams!' sang the crowd. 'There's only three David Beckhams!' and the older Beckham stood up and waved on the giant screen, laughing at the chant ringing round the ground.

Both had 'Beckham' emblazoned across the back of their shirts; during the extended half-time, the German team had followed England's example and now the iconic names on the German shirts more than explained why England were 3-0 down. The Greatest Ever England XI had been playing the All-Time World XI, each one of them the greatest player in their position ever to have lived, from Pelé up front to Lev Yashin between the sticks.

The news that Germany had cloned and trained the best players from all around the world had thrown up all sorts of philosophical and metaphysical questions which had rather stretched the intellectual powers of the pundits at half-time.

'So, Barry, FIFA are meeting to decide whether clones of Brazilian and Italian football stars born and raised in Germany should be permitted to play for the German national team. Any thoughts?'

'Well, Ron, it's a tough one, isn't it? On the one hand, the nation state is a social construct, a political tool built on collective myths and discredited notions of race and ethnicity, while on the other hand, yer can't have Pelé playing for the Krauts, that's a diabolical liberty, innit?'

I had returned to the press box where I'd watched the first half, but this time there had been a standing ovation from all the other journalists as I had taken my seat. My first hard-earned exposé had made me a pariah. The second, the one handed to me on a plate, put me on a list of the All-Time World's Greatest Journalists (Bernstein and Woodward up front, me playing in a four-man midfield with Walter Cronkite, George Orwell and Hunter S. Thompson). I felt my mobile phone vibrate in my pocket. It was a text from Tom. It simply said *Come On England! :-)*

That smiley face made my heart soar, three little punctuation marks arranged in such a way as to express love, forgiveness and his youthful optimism that England could yet win.

'Yeah . . .' I said out loud. 'Come on, England! We can still do this!'

The extended delays had had the unexpected effect of turning the second half into an evening match, the floodlights had lit up right at the moment that we had learnt that it was game on. Flares had been lit and smoke had drifted across the stands as the two greatest teams ever to be assembled emerged for this historic second half. And even though their own team was currently losing 3-0, the English fans cheered each name as the corrected German team sheet was read out. In goal: Lev Yashin. In defence: Maldini, Cafu, Beckenbauer and Santos; in midfield: Puskás, Cruyff, Beckham and Zidane, with Péle and Maradona playing up front. An hour's delay had been nothing like long enough for everyone to debate who they thought should have made it to the final team.

'I can't believe they've left out Eusébio!' exclaimed Bill, genuinely annoyed at the selection for the All-Time World XI. 'And you gotta have Messi in there; I'd play him at the top of a diamond with Garrincha and Dalglish on either side.'

Bill carried on listing legends they 'definitely should have included'. And his selection probably would have won, but mainly because it would have contained twenty-seven players.

But Messi had risen to fame too late to be included in the cloning programme, Brazil's Ronaldo just lost out on the basis of his 1998 World Cup final performance. Many of the other suggestions on everyone's lips were currently sitting on the German bench hoping to make one last World Cup appearance, alongside a whole cast of amazing footballers of every colour and ethnicity. During the earlier rounds each of us had privately thought, 'Wow, that's a very multi-racial team, considering it's Germany.' But nobody had had the nerve to say this out loud for fear of sounding racist on several fronts at once.

Thrilled though the crowd were to see these superstars playing together before their eyes, the atmosphere in the stadium had definitely changed, just as Blatter had intended. Now the English clearly were the underdogs; there was something heroically amateur about the nation who had pioneered the scientific breakthrough but had still tried to stick within the traditional rules. Every England kick was met with a huge cheer from the neutrals around the ground; the body language of the England team suggested pride rather than shame; even if they lost this evening, nobody would blame them.

And this was clearly liberating for the players; you could almost see the pressure being lifted from their shoulders, the way they were now enjoying their football; making brave, surprising passes and working that extra bit harder in the way that's only possible when you are really fired up. If I was to attempt to calculate the amount the England team were giving it, I would have estimated it to be pretty much bang on 110 per cent.

Five minutes into the half, Gordon Banks rolled the ball out to Bobby Moore, who carried the ball forward twenty yards, glancing up at his options left and right; his shirt still looking immaculate and freshly pressed as always, no matter how many times he had slid through mud and grass. With Pelé pressing, Moore laid it off to Stanley Matthews, who skipped past Zidane on the right wing, and with a burst of speed outpaced Cruyff to play a perfect pass to Bobby Charlton on the edge of the D. Bobby took a slight sidestep to send Beckenbauer the wrong way, and then smashed a cannonball shot from outside the area towards the top left corner of the goal.

'Yes!' I said leaping up. 'Goooooaaaaalllllll! Come on, England!'

I desperately wanted someone to celebrate with. I wish Tom had been there to punch the air beside me or Mark to predict that Charlton would probably follow it up with an own goal for the Germans.

'That was classic Charlton!' I said to the various hacks in the seats around me, and they nodded and put my quote into their match reports.

'Just like his goal against Portugal in '66,' I said, and I felt a little pleased with myself as they wrote that down as well. Now it felt like we were back in the game. 'Three-one!' I proclaimed. 'Well, that's the same as two-nil, isn't it?' They were about to write that down too but then thought better of it.

Germany were slow to restart, there seemed to be

some sort of argument between Pelé and Maradona about who should kick off. The tension between these two had been growing ever since they had been outed; it was almost as if they were both expecting the other to defer – to acknowledge who was the greatest player of all time.

'Next time, give the ball to me!'

'Oh yeah?' scoffed Maradona. 'And what are you ever gonna do?'

'Well I go on to become Minister for Sport. You become a coke addict.'

There were also rumours that, despite all efforts to make the team feel thoroughly German, some latent nationalist tensions had started to surface within the squad. Puskás had criticized Yashin for the brutal suppression of the 1956 Hungary uprising, Beckenbauer had intervened, prompting the Russian to accuse Hungary of being a fascist German client state. It could have got nasty if Beckham hadn't spoken up to break the tension. It wasn't what he said, they just laughed at his voice.

But now that their identities were out in the open, it was as if they were consciously trying to reclaim their heritage; each of them playing in a distinctive manner of their true country of origin. Practised without the cooperation of the rest of the team, Cruyff's 'Total Football' was simply 'Being out of Position All of the

Time'. Zinedine Zidane showed a certain amount of consistency by head-butting an Italian during a World Cup final. But the referee missed this incident and refused to believe that Maldini was injured, since the Italian had rolled around on the ground in agony every time anyone had so much as brushed against him.

With Germany still arguing amongst themselves, England pressed again; Duncan Edwards threading an impossible cross-field ball on to Gascoigne, who held off a challenge from Djalma Santos and squared to Keegan. Stanley Matthews was calling for it on the right, and Keegan feinted to pass to him, sending both German defenders the wrong way, passing instead to Lineker approaching on his left who now had a clear shot on goal. Lineker was one on one with the keeper! He was a certainty to score! I was standing up, almost cheering already . . . but what was Lineker doing? Instead of shooting he laid it off to the red shirt running into the box on his left, and there was Bobby Moore, the England captain, who blasted home from the edge of the eighteen-yard box! 'Goal!' I screamed. And not just any goal, but Bobby Moore's first ever England goal in a competitive match! Lineker could have scored himself but handed the chance to the England legend, and now the two embraced as Keegan grabbed the ball from the back of the net to run back and do it all over again.

'COME ON, ENGLAND! COME ON, ENGLAND!' roared the fans behind Gordon Banks, and Gascoigne turned and applauded the supporters. England looked like they could win this game on adrenalin alone; the energy and self-belief pumping through England's veins was surely going to get them level within minutes.

Which was when Diego Maradona suddenly collapsed in the centre circle after an innocuous challenge and then stayed there for five whole minutes, clutching different parts of either leg, depending on what the physios were asking him. The referee called for the stretcher, but in his agony, Maradona rolled away from it. He was helped to his feet, he collapsed again. The atmosphere was subsiding, the sting had been taken out of the match, Germany had time to consult their manager and regroup.

Now Germany kept eleven men behind the ball, they passed cautiously across the back of their half; although there were a whole thirty minutes to go, they seemed content to sit on their lead and simply kill the game dead. In his frustration, Gascoigne made a clumsy tackle and got a yellow card. England needed to make a substitution and now Gazza was the obvious player to take off. His face flushed red and his bottom lip quivered as he saw his number held up, he wiped his eyes on his shirt, and then ran off applauding the fans; tears were streaming down his face. 'Tears of a clone', I wrote in my match report.

Several players had been warming up on the touch-line. Glenn Hoddle was stretching and jogging. Bryan Robson had tripped over his laces and broken his collarbone but was now trying to 'run it off'. Tom Finney was smoking a pipe. But it was the maestro Johnny Haynes who came on for Gascoigne, patting his Brylcreemed hair into place as he jogged into position with a mission to reignite the England team. With Haynes, Stanley Matthews and Bobby Charlton in the midfield, it felt like I should be watching this bit of the game in black and white; with a laughing policeman striding past swathes of wizened male supporters, all flat caps and bad teeth, smoking roll-ups and waving rattles.

But the stoppage had lost England their momentum. The crowd had gone quiet and England seemed to have run out of energy and ideas. I could feel the adrenalin seeping away: it was as if we had been allotted our time to score the equalizer but that phase of the game was now over. Five minutes passed, then ten. Neither side looked likely to score and the Germans were happy with that. I felt my phone vibrate in my pocket. 'Who the hell is calling me in the middle of the World Cup final?' I said out loud. 'What can possibly be more im-portant than *this* game *right now*!' I exclaimed. But the caller ID was flashing with the name of my son. I was never going to reject a call from him.

'Dad? Dad? Are you there?'

The line was weak, the noise around me made him even fainter. I leapt out of my seat and headed to the doors of the Press Suite, with Bill Butler looking at me as if I must have lost my mind.

'Hang on, Tom, let me just go where I can hear you . . .'

'Dad, we have to turn this around, we have to get another goal . . .'

He said it as if this observation might be news to me; as if this wasn't quite an obvious statement.

'I know, son, but I'm not sure they've got anything left to give . . .'

Now I was on the inside of the Press Suite, out of view of the pitch. It was completely deserted; not even the hospitality staff were missing the match of the century.

'That's why I'm calling, Dad . . . The England fans have gone all quiet, they're sitting down; you have to get over there and do what we did at Wembley . . .'

'What?'

'Get in amongst the England fans and start singing like we did against Poland! Germany have all the best players in the entire history of the world, Dad. England don't stand a chance unless we have the best fans!'

'But . . . but . . . I'm supposed to be covering the game from my press seat; I don't have a seat over there . . .'

'Dad! No one should be sitting anyway.'

The certainty in his voice was very persuasive. My pass allowed me all over the ground; there was nothing to stop me heading over to the England section. 'I'll call you back,' I said abruptly and hung up.

Five minutes later I took up a position at the top of a stairway in the middle of the subdued England supporters. Then I called my son back. 'Sing it, Tom! I've put you on speakerphone – sing what we sang against Poland!'

And I held my phone in the air and a few fans looked around to see where that tinny unbroken voice was coming from, as back in England Tom half-sang, half-shouted, 'Stand up! If you still believe! Stand up! If you still believe . . .'

Then the face of a big bald bloke on the end of the row seemed to register a memory of that night at Wembley, and he looked at me and gave an almost imperceptible nod. He stood up and together we began singing 'Stand up! If you still believe . . .' gently at first, and then more emphatically. And then two people beside him joined in, and then others in front and behind, and suddenly it was like a fire in a dry cornfield, spreading in all directions; the clatter of seats flipping back as tens of thousands stood and shouted their faith in their team as loud as they possibly could.

'Listen to that, Tom!' I shouted into the phone, then holding it up in the air. 'Listen to what you have started!'

But it was too loud to talk to him any more. I couldn't tell if he could hear it, but I could tell for certain that the players did. The demeanour of the England players changed, their heads were up again, they were passing forward instead of back.

Now Matthews went on a dizzying dribble down the right wing, drawing defenders across field and collecting so many opposition players around him that I expected the German manager to shout, 'Boys, stop bunching!' At exactly the right moment he laid it off to Haynes, who wafted a perfect pass across the entire width of the pitch to where Ashley Cole had made a run into the acres of space on the left. Showing far better judgement than he did in his relationship with Cheryl, Cole opted to pass to Lineker in the six-yard box, who trapped the ball on his thigh, swivelled and blasted a shot which already had me standing and cheering a goal.

But no, Yashin had saved it! It was pushed on to the crossbar where it spun up into the air towards Pelé, who was ready to collect it on the edge of the eighteen-yard box. It takes a really great player to have the confidence to do what Pelé did next; only someone of his ability and composure would even attempt such a move in a crowded goalmouth. Pelé calmly headed the ball back towards the keeper. No one was expecting it. Least of all his goalkeeper, who scrambled back across his goalmouth and then watched the ball sail over his head into the corner of the goal.

There was a confused split second before the stadium erupted. England were level! They had returned from the dead and had got it back to 3-3, thanks to the England fans' exultations and a bizarre own goal from Pelé. Even the very greatest players can make silly little mistakes sometimes.

Despite the euphoria of the moment, nobody was quite sure how to celebrate. Beckham ran and hugged Lineker, and then tried to hug Haynes and Stanley Matthews, who had no intention of kissing and cuddling other grown men in such an undignified and unmanly fashion. No, a quick handshake and pat on the back and then a brisk jog back to the centre circle was all that was required. I noticed Bobby Charlton offer a few sympathetic words to Pelé before the restart. 'It could happen to any of us, mate,' was apparently what he said. 'You're still the greatest player in the history of football.' What wonderful sportsmanship, I thought. And making sure he said it loud enough for Maradona to overhear, that was an excellent wind-up along the way.

I got a text from Tom: *We did that!* I sent a message back: *No, YOU did that!* and then another text saying: *And don't worry, I'm staying right here.* But now the noise in the stadium was louder than anything I had ever heard at a football match. 'England! England!' It was lucky they hadn't closed the roof, because it would have been lifted off by the force of the England chanting by now. Qatar had built an eighty thousand all-seater stadium especially for this match, and not a single person was left sitting down.

Germany decided it was time for them to make a substitution and I worried at the seemingly infinite array of talent available to them. Their choice crystallized the emotional conflict I had felt throughout this game – acutely aware of the privilege of just being there and watching so many great players, but still hoping they might not be at their very greatest when they were playing my team. A huge cheer went up from both sets of supporters as the giant screen showed the name of the next player to come on. 'At last!' I shouted. 'At last he gets to play in a World Cup!' as the distinctive long hair and sideburns of Georgie Best made their debut, his fingers clutching the cuffs of his shirt as they had done so often before. I was delighted and terrified at the same time.

I wanted to witness George Best's audacity, his confidence, I wanted to see him beat three defenders, but then put his shot a good ten yards wide at the end of it. George Best was something of a soccer superstar back in Germany, married as he was to Miss Germany, the 2021 winner of Miss World.* Despite his undisputed genius as a footballer, he struck me as a risky character to put on when the game was so finely balanced. How could Germany be sure which George Best they were going to get? The dazzling player who starred in Manchester United's European Cup triumph, or the petulant pop star who failed to turn up for training and kept threatening to quit the game? I had spotted Best swigging from a water bottle before he ran on. I stared hard at the giant screen to check there wasn't ice and lemon in it.

Almost immediately Best had an impact; running at speed at defenders, dribbling through a maze of players and somehow still emerging with the ball at his feet to shoot. His second strike forced Gordon Banks into an astonishing reaction save; for a split second I had been convinced that a German-speaking Irish lad from the Loyalist half of Belfast had put England out of the World Cup final.

The last twenty minutes of the game sped by, with both sides having several chances to win it. Johan

---

*Although it later emerged that Miss Germany was in fact a clone of the 1998 winner Miss Sweden.

Cruyff hit the bar, while the English David Beckham almost chipped Yashin from sixty yards. Stuart Pearce came on for Cole and promptly stopped Pelé running through on goal; it took you right back to the days of Bobby Moore, who had done something similar ten minutes earlier.

The game of all games looked set to go to extra time; by now more players were walking than running. The four added minutes had been played and we were into the abstract philosophical meta-time known as 'time added on to time added on'. My knotted stomach twisted even further as Maradona nearly scored with his hand, but Stuart Pearce used his hand to stop the ball crossing the line. With no irony whatsoever, Maradona adopted an air of outrage and indignation that an England player had handballed his own handled shot. 'I wasn't going to let him get away with that a second time!' laughed Pearce in an interview later.

As the final whistle blew, the German team sank to the ground exhausted while Alf Ramsey ordered the English players to stay on their feet. Normally I would have used these precious minutes to jot down the key incidents for my match report, but having found a place to stand in the middle of the England supporters, I wasn't going to watch extra time anywhere else.

I tried to call Tom again, but I couldn't get through; even texts were failing to send now that everyone in the stadium was trying to contact loved ones. But it gave me a moment to pause and take it all in – how lucky I was to be here at this extraordinary game and to watch it with ordinary fans.

England had thirty minutes to score a goal or face the Germans in a penalty shoot-out. And everyone knows what happens when England face Germany in a penalty shoot-out. 'One Englishman always misses a penalty,' as Mark would say, though for once he wasn't being unduly pessimistic. Sometimes it was *two* Englishmen. We had to get a goal in open play; to get through extra time in the World Cup final and lose it on penalties would be too cruel.

To that end Keegan was now replaced by Stan Mortensen; the first player to score for England at a World Cup.

Mortensen kicked off and tapped it to Lineker who knocked it back to Beckham. The German David Beckham then charged him down and England won a foul. Beckham was lying on the ground, and for a moment I feared he might kick out at his alter ego, and get himself sent off, as it were. Beckham took the kick quickly, so quickly in fact that none of his team were expecting it, and now Germany were in possession. Beckenbauer, the German captain, played a quick one-two with Puskás. Maldini had found some space on the right and laid it off to Beckenbauer, who somehow seemed to have switched to midfield. It all happened so quickly, some people were still taking their seats as Pelé, Zidane and Cruyff passed quickly up field and finally laid the ball off to Beckenbauer who blasted a shot that was beyond Banks' reach and suddenly the wrong section of the ground erupted into rapture.

Only one minute of extra time played and we were losing again. And in an instant it was five minutes of extra time played, and then ten, and we were still losing. They changed ends after fifteen minutes but annoyingly Germany remembered to aim for the opposite goal. And I made a pact with fate that I would happily settle for penalties. 'There is nothing England like more than a penalty shoot-out against the Germans! Definitely – penalties would be great.'

The England fans tried to start up with the magic song once more, but you can't pull a second rabbit out of a hat and expect the same reaction. Even though the fans maintained the noise levels, England's frustration was showing. They were shooting from too far out, or losing possession with over-optimistic lobs up field. I started to prepare myself for defeat – England had performed magnificently after all, it was the greatest game of football ever played. Perhaps at some profound level the English people might actually prefer coming second; like Scott of the Antarctic, there's something heroically British about losing with honour.

And then the fourth official was holding up the board to indicate that we were now playing a minimum of one minute of time added on and the German fans were singing 'Football's Coming Home' which struck me as unnecessarily mocking.

Time for one last attack from England! The red shirts passed around the German half but couldn't break through. Then a clumsy challenge from Zidane won England a free kick. It was a good forty yards out, but it was a chance. More time was wasted as the Germans lined up their defenders.

Cometh the hour, cometh the clone. David Beckham stepped up to take the impossible kick. He's never scored from this far out, I thought; he'd do better to lay it off to Stan Mortensen running into the box. There was a cacophony of whistles from the German fans; terrified silence from the England end. The referee, who had clearly studied mime, was still over-acting the motion of moving a wall back to where he had sprayed his line of shaving foam.

Eighty thousand people were focused on one man looking down at a football. He glanced across to the VIP seats, did he momentarily make eye contact with the original David Beckham? Then he glanced up and ran at the ball and struck it with all his might. On the end of the wall, Beckenbauer leapt, but it flew past his head, no, no, it was going wide, it was going wide . . .

But within that split second my mind went from disappointment to hope that it might be bending and then astonishment at the amount of curve he had managed to put on the ball; it hit the inside of the post; it flew across the goalmouth; it hit the opposite post and then it spun into the back of the net.

'YEEEEESSSSSSSSSSSS! GOOOOAAALLLLL!' There are not many situations in our lives when it feels perfectly normal to hug a complete stranger.

'GOOALLLLLLL! DAVID BECKHAM!!!! BACK OF THE NET!'

A last-gasp equalizer from David Beckham, defying the laws of physics to bend it round the wall to get England level in the last second of the World Cup final. I watched it over and over again on the giant screen: the curve on that shot was like an impossible magic trick, in another age he'd be burnt at the stake for witchcraft.

ENGLAND 4 GERMANY 4 said the giant digital scoreboard. David Beckham had disappeared under a pile of England players, which always strikes me as a strange way to reward a goal scorer: crush and suffocate him and risk him taking no further part in the season.

Four-four in extra time, penalties looming in the most incredible World Cup final of all time – and there's still one bloke a few rows in front of you who thinks, 'This would be a good time to leave so that I don't get caught up in the traffic . . .'

'Can't we stay and see who wins, Dad?'

'No, let's beat the rush for the exits . . .'

Perhaps he couldn't bear to watch the Russian roulette of penalties; every football fan has their own way of coping. Some look away, others cover their eyes. I think some England penalty-takers look away and cover their eyes. Our record in this aspect of the game was abysmal and now, when the final whistle blew, I prepared myself for the worst with the consoling thought that whatever happened next, the greatest football players in the history of the world had not been able to beat England in open play.

Obviously the complex notion of players taking turns to kick a ball from the penalty spot takes forever to organize. A Qatari coin was tossed, but it turned out there was just squiggly writing on both sides, so they had to find another coin from somewhere else. I studied the body language of the England players, which of them looked up for it; who was hiding behind a teammate as the list was drawn up. I imagined the atmosphere in pubs across England; small, nervous sips from pints of lager; footy fans at home sitting on the arm of the sofa because to sit in it properly might suggest casual half-interest. 'I can't believe England don't practise for penalty shoot-outs,' I said to anyone who was listening. I got a text message from Mark: *So right about now you will be moaning about how they ought to practise for penalty shoot-outs.* Presumably his ex-girlfriend would be in a sports bar somewhere asking if they could switch one of the screens over to Animal Planet.

Eleven sweat-soaked England players stood in the centre circle, and eventually Gary Lineker peeled away and began the lonely walk to the penalty spot. Lineker didn't bother with any sort of mind games, languidly adjusting his boots or repeatedly repositioning the ball. He put it down on the spot, took a few steps back and then kicked the ball very, very hard in the direction of the goal. In that second I felt such enormous gratitude to Gary Lineker for successfully scoring a penalty, like he had done me a huge personal favour.

The back of the net seemed to be directly wired up to all the England fans behind the goal. Every one of them was motionless and silent, but the moment the ball hit the netting they exploded in screams of joy. Now Gordon Banks faced his first opponent. First up for Germany was Pelé. He was quite good, wasn't he?

Pelé scored. The German fans cheered wildly, one or two of them had brought vuvuzelas, which was surely reason enough to hand the World Cup to England right now. Stan Mortensen scored for England, and then Beckenbauer for his country. I had no more nails left to bite, I didn't know what to do with my arms, I had to stop myself holding hands with the fat, bald bloke next to me. Next came Stuart Pearce, who had famously missed a penalty in Italia 90, but then had had the courage to take another at Euro 96. He scored again and screamed at the England fans like he was one of them. Neither keeper was even getting close to any of these. If a penalty is struck with enough force at the right part of the goal, not even a goalie guessing the right way can stop it. Apart from that quite important factor, there is apparently, no point in practising penalties.

Then came George Best. He ran, slowed down, and dinked a cheeky chip over the sprawling Gordon Banks to make it 3-3. Someone had to make a mistake soon. Next up was the England captain Bobby Moore.

'Oh, don't let Bobby Moore miss,' I said out loud. 'Not Bobby Moore.' We were perfectly happy with the place of the late Bobby Moore in our national iconography – the image of him clutching the Jules Rimet trophy above his head, carried on the shoulders of his England teammates – we didn't want that replaced by a picture of failure and disappointment. But Yashin dived the right way! He got his fingertips to the ball, it hit the post! And then it bounced off the goalie's head and went in.

The German players surrounded the referee. 'That's a miss!' they claimed. 'In a penalty shoot-out, there are no rebounds or second chances . . .' There was a moment of uncertainty until the referee waved them away. 'Off the post and in off the keeper' counts as a goal. 'Off the post and back in from the striker' doesn't count. Both sides still had a 100 per cent record and Bobby Moore jogged back to his teammates, modestly applauding the fans singing his name.

Maradona scored his penalty and then his screaming face went running up close to a pitchside TV camera, as a FIFA official made a mental note to have him tested for drugs later. But this penalty was the turning point. Maradona had powered a shot straight down the middle and Banks had stayed on his feet. The seventy-mile-an-hour ball hit Banks square in the face, leaving him sprawled inside his own goal clutching his face as blood ran over his gloves. There was some delay and he was still being given medical attention while David Beckham scored England's fifth.

It was effectively sudden death; England were 5-4 up, so if Germany missed now, we would be World Champions. But our goalkeeper was looking doubtful. A wet sponge was roughly rubbed all over his face, but it did not reset the broken bone in his nose or reverse the concussion. Banks was out of the game. England asked if they could put on their reserve goalie Peter Shilton, but were curtly informed that they had used all their substitutes.

'That's ridiculous,' said the bloke in front of me, 'the referee's definitely got that one wrong.'

'No, those are actually the rules,' said his friend. 'The referee's right, just like he was about the ball in off Yashin's head.'

'That's all very well, but what about a bit of common sense?'

Down on the pitch the arguments continued for some time. It would have to be one of the outfield players still on the pitch. Bobby Moore had the players all together in the centre circle; the talk was animated and urgent. Around me were the discordant voices of confused supporters speculating and guessing what might happen next. A helicopter was hovering way above the stadium, and on the giant screen we saw the aerial night shot of the little stadium with the tiny figures down on the green square, looking so insignificant and incidental.

Then from inside a huddle of England players emerged David Beckham. He pulled off his red shirt, revealing his tattooed torso, soaked with sweat and shining under the floodlights. A huge cheer grew all around the ground, flashlights sparkling in the night. Beckham was going in goal for England! He walked across the pitch with his top off; fortunately the referee was not such a stickler for the rules to give him a yellow card. In the goalmouth he was thrown a green jersey and he kicked the back of his boots against the goalposts in the way that he had seen proper goalies do.

David Beckham had already taken his penalty and scored. But fate had decided that the next German player to take a penalty was their own David Beckham. German Beckham began the long walk to the penalty spot. English Beckham allowed himself a wry smile as he saw whose shot he was going to have to try and stop.

'Two David Beckhams! There's only two David Beckhams!' came the chant around the ground again.

Beckham and Beckham stood twelve yards apart, German Beckham now trying to avoid eye contact.

'You're an Englishman, David!' shouted the goalkeeper to his blood brother. 'You're an Englishman just like me.'

German Beckham placed the ball on the penalty spot.

'And you know what? One Englishman always misses a penalty!'

Did German Beckham wince slightly at that?

'One Englishman always misses a penalty, but it's OK because tonight he's playing for Germany . . .'

Germany's number 7 finally looked up and made eye contact with his opponent. If he missed this, England would win the World Cup. He turned and looked at the two teams standing way back on the halfway line. He smiled at English Beckham standing there with his arms outstretched; jumping slightly on the spot. And then German Beckham ran up and kicked the ball with all his might.

It rocketed over the bar and way up into the stands behind.

Winners

Junction Juniors v Junction Juniors
Impromptu kick-about
Bishops Common – 20 December 2022

In that moment when England won the World Cup final I knew that all the personal problems of my whole life had been instantly and magically solved. Millions of England fans felt the same thing, that's why we were all cheering so wildly. Niggling health worry? Finally cured. That ongoing marital fault line? Suddenly resolved. Increasing debt issues? Not a problem; just spend two grand on a season ticket and you forget all about it for ninety minutes every Saturday. Strangers were hugging one another in the stadium or in pubs back home, because we all shared that once-in-a-lifetime joy, the relief that this universal panacea had put right everything that was wrong. England were champions of the world. In that moment, nothing else mattered.

My only regret about the moment for which I'd

waited my entire life was that I could only experience it once. Of course there was no better place to be than in the stadium itself, but I'm rather counting on those scientists who developed human clones to invent time travel as well, so I can go back and experience it over and over again with all the friends and family with whom I have shared football down the decades.

I'd watch England win the World Cup in the pub against the expectations of pessimistic Mark, in the midst of the crowd who'd witnessed all the disappointments and 'what-ifs' down the decades. I'd watch it at home with Tom and pizza delivered as a treat, and Tom going out and running up and down the street with his England scarf when the World Cup was won. Or we might invite all of Tom's friends round, the entire squad of Junction Juniors, and inscrutably I would watch the disappointment on their young faces as England went 3-0 down, and then see the hope grow during the second half until all that shaken-up fizzy tension exploded the moment Germany's final penalty went flying over the bar. And then I would have watched it back in the stadium, spending the whole game in amongst all the England fans who had saved all that money and used up their holiday leave to follow their heroes around the world, and finally been rewarded with the greatest comeback in the greatest sporting event in the history of the world.

The newsfeeds in Qatar had shown the reaction back in England, from cameras placed in packed sports bars and from the giant screens that had been erected in town squares around the land. Tears on the face-paint of that young lad when England had let in that third goal; the jubilation in the crowds when we got back to three-all. Cut to a pretty girl in an England shirt biting her lip (no sports director graduates from film school without learning you have to cut to a pretty girl in a football shirt biting her lip). And then that moment, the moment that England won it!

A single penalty kick, just over the bar or just under the bar; that was the tiny margin between ecstasy and despair; a single shot on goal taken three thousand miles from home that transformed the mood of an entire nation. Although I clearly saw the ball fly over the bar, I remember feeling a split second of uncertainty – as if the referee might order the penalty to be retaken or worrying that I might have somehow miscounted. But German Beckham had missed and English Beckham had thrown his arms in the air and was running to his teammates and yes, yes, we had done it – look at the celebrations on the pitch, listen to the England fans in the stadium, England really had won!

The other British journalists in the press area had dropped their professional cool and were jumping up and down along with me. Other nationalities were applauding and smiling for us, knowing that they had been privileged to witness a truly epic World Cup final. It was hard to think of anything that could have made that match any more exciting, more meaningful or mythic. Maybe if some England fans had invaded the pitch just before the last penalty? Then the commentator could have said 'Some people are on the pitch, they think it's all over!' Except that the security levels in Qatar were pretty extreme; anyone running on to the pitch would have been beaten with batons and then had mace sprayed in their face by the private militia, and that might have diminished the joyful exuberance of it all.

The fans chanted the names of their heroes in turn, who acknowledged the supporters with applause of their own. The players shook hands with the exhausted and emotionally drained opposition; Pelé came up to Bobby Moore and embraced the victorious captain. I was clapping so hard my hands hurt, and eventually the players climbed those un-famous forty-seven steps to collect the World Cup and their medals from the dignitaries.

There was Prince William, President of the FA, maybe showing the first signs of baldness now in 2022. There was Michel Platini, enjoying his last appearance as FIFA President before his role as a front man for the real Mr Big was finally exposed. And there was the

Emir of Qatar who had of course played in this tournament himself and learnt that it's not the winning that counts (even though he had won something himself – an online poll on the worst player ever to appear at the World Cup finals).

When Bobby Moore held the World Cup above his head I was too emotionally drained to cheer any louder than I had been for hours. This was *the photo*, this was the image; but then so was the moment when the German team had formed a guard of honour to applaud the winners up towards the steps and so was the moment when Prince William punched his fist in the air, having passed the World Cup to the England captain. In the post-match interview, the England manager Alf Ramsey remained typically understated and said, 'This was a most satisfactory result, and I am pleased with the considerable effort put in by the players.' His dignified, some would say haughty, manner was not really designed to accommodate Paul Gascoigne rushing into the shot and pouring champagne all over his head.

Another interview with Bobby Charlton touched on how the players felt, now that their true identities were out in the open. 'It's a bit of a relief, to be honest. I'm glad that fella published his story. Means we can just be who we are and get on with playing football.'

'Did the discovery of who you were really up against at half-time transform the psychology of the England team?'

'Yeah, I think it did. We realized we were up against the eleven greatest individuals. And the only way you can counter that is by being a better team.'

The following day Paul Gascoigne set off the metal detector at the airport and a quick once-over with the hand-held scanner revealed that he had a World Cup trophy tucked inside his jacket. The players arrived home to a besieged airport, a bit like when Ayatollah Khomeini returned to Tehran, only with more religious fervour. It seemed like half the population of England had been drawn to the historic, national monument that was Luton Airport.

'Why are you here?' asked a TV reporter to a face-painted family in England shirts.

'To see the England team.'

Good to have cleared that up. I had flown back on an earlier plane, but already there had been banks of photographers and news crews waiting. 'I wonder if any of them will want to talk to me?' I wondered; *The man who broke the football story of the century?* I walked straight past without them so much as noticing me. The narrative of the news demands victims, villains and occasional heroes. I was never the first; no longer the second, and they had far bigger heroes to focus on now. But meeting Suzanne and Tom at the arrivals lounge was my own private victorious return. 'I'm so proud of you,' said the mother of my son. 'You played a blinder.'

It was the first time we'd properly embraced since Tom had been born.

'I'm glad you ran that story, Dad,' said my son on the way home.

'Yeah . . . I reckon Germany would have won otherwise.'

'No, I meant because it was *true*.'

In any case I had already received a congratulatory email from the chief editor at the *Mirror* saying he was relaunching the paper's football supplement and would I like to edit it? And the long-overdue book I was supposed to be writing on the greatest ever England players, well it ended up being a very different book to the one I had started, as you might have noticed now that you've nearly finished it.

That night Tom wanted to stay over with me and finally we got to watch the World Cup highlights together. Tom was wearing the official England shirt I had brought home for him; through a contact with the FA, I had managed to get it signed by every member of the team. And a week later I put it in the wash, and wished I had used indelible ink. Mark joined us for the highlights of the second half and penalties.

'See this is why there's no point in practising penalty shoot-outs,' he explained to Tom. 'Facing a goalie who is a clone of yourself yet from another country. You can't recreate that situation on the training ground . . .'

'I still can't believe it,' I said to myself. 'England have won the World Cup!'

'Yeah, but we'll never retain it.'

I took Tom and all his friends from Junction Juniors to see the victory parade through central London; an excited gaggle of eleven-year-olds in matching England shirts, all clasping little plastic St George's flags that said *Made in China* on the handle. Drivers let us cross, taxi drivers tooted their horns, strangers in the capital city were acknowledging one another. We settled on a great vantage point on the Mall and pointed out the jokes on the banners and the fans up in the trees. And looking down the Mall towards Buckingham Palace I noticed a curious thing. Obviously there were hundreds of Union flags and St George's flags and the odd red or blue ensign or Three Lions towels tied to a stick for the occasion. But in amongst them, I also spotted the flags of many other countries: Australia, Jamaica, the United States, Sweden, Ghana and Poland. This was the tournament when I came to understand that nationalism had moved on since my childhood; these guest flags seemed to say 'We've come along to be part of this great English celebration, to say *well done, England*, from the people of other countries who all love living here.' You can be an English Swede who loves both countries, you can be a London Kiwi who cheers for England in football and the All Blacks in rugby, you can be proud of all the different parts of your culture and heritage just as parents are proud of their different children in varying ways. You can be a German Pelé if you want to be. You can play for the Republic of Ireland and have an English accent. Oh – actually you could always do that. I chatted to a bloke with a London accent waving a Greek flag. His name was Nick and he supported Spurs and Panathinaikos. Beyond him was an Asian-looking man waving two little flags, an England one and a white cross on a black background.

'What country is that one?' I asked him.

'That is Cornwall,' he said proudly. Obviously. Patriotism is simple; you can be proud of anything and anywhere – just don't ever use it to denigrate anyone else.

The bus came through Admiralty Arch and a huge cheer came down the Mall like a wave of sound. It could have been VE Day or a Royal Wedding, it didn't really matter, it was simply an occasion for all of us to come together and feel as one and part of something bigger than our normal lives. And from the top of the bus David Beckham looked directly at our group and gave Junction Juniors the thumbs up. He'd obviously never seen them play. I remembered the slight surprise I must have shown when Sepp Blatter had named David Beckham in the All-Time World XI. Blatter acknowledged my raised eyebrow by saying, 'This has been an incredibly expensive business. I think they will need to sell a lot of shirts after this.'

Eventually we all headed home and after sandwiches and sugary drinks of dubious colours, the boys debated what they should do now. Tom grabbed a ball and after a few texts and calls, there was a whole crowd of them heading up the road. Like the boys themselves, the ball was too big and bouncy to be played with here on the pavement, it was not quite under control; it thudded off parked cars or rolled dangerously out into the road. But then on to the grass and they were off the lead; they kicked the ball ahead and chased after it, carelessly dropping bags and jackets as they ran. And on the same common where they had cried as seven-year-old nascent footballers, on the very grass where they had feared the approach of the enormous ball, or struggled to comprehend the angry shouts of parents from the touchline; now these same boys played their own game of football. Just themselves, against each other; no league points to be won, no school cup to be knocked out of; just a dozen friends and a ball and a flat bit of grass. I so would have loved to join in and play with them, but they didn't need me any more. They casually arranged themselves into two teams, and found some traffic cones and an old crate to make goalposts. And then they played for hours.

It was not the most disciplined game of football ever seen. With no pitch markings, the wingers found that they had more space than usual on the flanks, like halfway to Canada. On one occasion a near miss did not rebound off the woodwork but sent the goalpost flying like a skittle, leading to fervent debate as to whether or not a goal had been scored 'in-off'. Since the team claiming the goal was losing by the unusual scoreline of 23-18, it was decided to allow the goal to stand. The restart was then delayed further by the scorer doing a goal celebration of putting two traffic cones to his chest and impersonating a well-known female singer. The goalkeeper laughed so much he had to lie on the ground, which was the cue for another player to drench him with his water bottle, which became the default goal celebration for the rest of the game and increased the motivation to score as much as any Premiership bonus.

And afterwards they went up to the bandstand café and I found them, drinking cans of Coke or lemonade, all red faces and wet fringes; laughing and chatting, reliving the best moments, the missed opportunities and the well-taken goals.

'We should have a kick-about every weekend.'

The proposal was greeted with great enthusiasm.

'Like we could meet at the bandstand at nine . . .'

The early kick-off; less so.

'Well, ten maybe . . .'

'Eleven o'clock. We could meet on the common at eleven.'

'Twelve o'clock. Noon by the bandstand. And I've got some proper goals, though they take a while to put up, so maybe – kick-off at one?'

'Yeah, even if we all end up at different secondary schools and that, we could still keep meeting up to play football together, like . . . *for ever*!'

And sitting there listening to them as their former and now redundant manager, I understood that finally Junction Juniors had won. The team that had barely even scored in a competitive game had come out on top. They had learnt to embrace football on their own terms; they played purely for the love of it, meeting up as friends to play together, not caring whether they were any good or not, no one under pressure to perform or to end up disappointed at being left on the bench; they just played. They'd always have football; their friendship had this vessel, this universal operating system that would keep bringing them back together week after week, year after year.

It only takes you a lifetime of playing football to realize that this is as precious as any World Cup winner's medal.

Acknowledgements

With thanks to the various friends and fellow writers who read earlier drafts and laughed at the notion of England getting to a World Cup final; especially Pete Sinclair (Scottish), John McNally (Welsh) and Karey Kirkpatrick (American). Enormous thanks to my family, Jackie, Freddie and Lily, who have indulged and shared my own love affair with football. And thanks also to Clint Dempsey for scoring with that eighty-second-minute chip to make the final score Fulham 5 Juventus 4. It made me very happy.